1

About three months ago...the end of March

Montgomery Ransom, known simply as Ransom, watched as the bartender showed *her* to a booth across from where he lingered near the opposite end of the bar chatting with Jon Vargas, Jon's girlfriend Angie Bennett, and her brother Mitch. However, Ransom's attention was hardly on the conversation. His concentration was on the woman who looked no further than the hostess stand when she entered. Every nerve in his body tingled with tension the instant she stepped foot into the restaurant. He didn't need to glance at the threshold for confirmation—although he had. There was something about her that his body instinctively reacted to.

He purposely made himself relax so Jon would not detect the change in Ransom's body language. They were familiar enough with each other for Jon to sense something was up. When you had been in enough...what was a suitable term? Maybe orgies would be the best term, although they didn't refer to them that way. Maybe sexual encounters was the better phrase. Hell, seeing *her* had jumbled his brain and he couldn't think clearly. When you have done—whatever the right word was—enough times with the same people as he and Jon had, it was easy to notice the change in someone's body language.

And if the tension in him wasn't enough confirmation of who the woman across the room was, there was no question when he considered her hair as she spoke with Tammy. The color of her hair was unique, but not outrageous; at least not anymore. He remembered pictures of her as a child and on through her teens with wavy, vivid orange colored hair that went just beyond her shoulder blades. An introduction to

1

a talented stylist transformed her hair into a stunning dark copper by adding darker shades of auburn and brown. The color resembled a penny that had been in circulation for a few years. He knew that in the usual redhead fashion she did not tan, but freckled. So, the golden color of her skin was a consequence of her freckles darkening. The dark purple sweater she had on beautifully enhanced her coloring and perfectly complemented the color of her hair. The fitted, off-white pants created the illusion of her legs being miles long. She often wore heels, determined to hide her true height. She was about five-foot-three, but he knew that the heels she frequently wore made her five-foot-five or taller.

She was now gazing out the window of his downtown Charleston restaurant, watching the crowds of people walk around, enjoying the exceptionally balmy March evening. She remained unaware of him observing her, which surprised him. In the past, she had been just as aware of him as he was of her. A piece of him silently pleaded for her to glance his way, to make eye contact with him. The rest of him fervently hoped that she wouldn't. He knew he couldn't resist her if she did. He would try, but he would fail.

He intercepted Tammy with a gesture as she neared him. "Tammy, what did she order?"

"A glass of pinot noir," she replied, not needing any clarification of who "she" was. It was Tammy's only table tonight, as she was manning the bar.

"Retrieve a bottle from my reserve instead," he said, passing her a key. He stored a few pricier wines under lock and key. "Bring it to me and I'll take it to her."

He had already failed in his resistance. He would go to her. He always would. She called him like the Lorelei she resembled. He would follow

LIAISONS

BOOK 3

Liaisons Book 3

H. Elizabeth Austin

Published by H. Elizabeth Austin

Distributed by Amazon Direct Publishing

Copyright 2024 by Heather Austin

Coverart design credit: Canva and H. Elizabeth Austin

License Notes

Thank you...

———

Writing is often a solitary job. Liaisons Book 3 was one of the more difficult to write, I think. Partially, because as you discover, it covered much of the time Liaisons Book 1 and 2 do. If you look at back to books 1 and 2 in the series, you didn't see a lot of Ransom, and now you will know why. What made this book hard to write was ensuring the timeline was correct and trying to build three months of tension but keeping the mystery element present but not predictable. This book has been over a year in the making.

As usual, I had a lot of sound boards as I wrote parts of this book. Lots of people go into the process of bringing this to you.

Beth, Jana, Li'l, and Bonnie thank you for your proofreading and editing. I appreciate it when you make me think about word choice. Switching my brain from professor mode to writer mode is often hard and I tend to initially use words that people don't use in everyday conversation.

Chris, my wonderful husband, what more can I say. You continue to talk about my books with everyone you meet and are helping me get more comfortable talking about them too. Thank you for all the support you've given me!

Finally, to the readers: You have no idea how I appreciate your support. I am honored to share my stories with you.

her to his death as the sailors in the poem once did when the Lorelei sang.

"Okay," Tammy replied, stretching out the syllables in a show of her confusion. He knew Tammy questioned why he asked for a much more expensive bottle of wine for someone who ordered only a glass of an already excellent wine. Tammy was well aware that he solely used his reserve wines to indulge a table of women or to pacify a customer who complained about the otherwise exceptional selection of wine the restaurant offered. He knew Tammy also wondered why because he had not even interacted with the woman. So why would he pull one of those bottles without having spoken to the woman yet? But Ransom didn't bother to share anything more with Tammy and Tammy wouldn't probe.

He redirected his focus back to the woman in the booth while holding on to a thread of the discussion between Jon, Angie, and Mitch.

Last Ransom had heard, the woman across the room was engaged. But from where he stood, he couldn't see a ring on her finger. He knew he shouldn't talk to her, but he couldn't stop himself from wanting to. She was his Achilles heel. No, she was his addiction. Worse than that. She was his everything. Hence the irresistible urge to go to her.

Tammy halted next to him with a bottle a short time later and returned the key he'd handed her earlier.

"Excuse me, I see an old friend I need to catch up with," he said to the group as he took the bottle and corkscrew from Tammy and strolled away before anyone in the group could reply. He sensed Jon's gaze following him as he walked away. There might be questions later, but he wasn't concerned about it. He wasn't doing anything he hadn't done many times before at the restaurant.

The scene outside still held her focus. Having heard him approach, she turned and cast a puzzled look at the bottle he placed on the table. Her gaze locked on his hand, gripping the bottle before it traveled up his arm, up to his shoulder, and moved over to his face.

"Ran!" she gasped as she drew in a sharp breath.

"Hello, Fi," he said, his voice low and intimate. "I thought you'd like this wine better." He inserted the corkscrew into the bottle without breaking eye contact with her and effortlessly removed the cork within seconds.

Tammy placed two glasses on the table and disappeared. As he examined Fiona's sapphire blue eyes, Ransom filled the wine glass—he had always had good peripheral vision. He never met anyone with eyes the same as hers. They were a deep, clear blue, but there was no mistaking the color. And they never changed color. "I wasn't aware you were in town," he remarked as he poured wine into the second glass before lowering himself onto the opposite bench of the booth.

"Please, sit," Fiona uttered. He could hear the thinly concealed sarcasm in her voice. Then she responded to his question. "I arrived yesterday. I'm here for a few months. I have a consulting contract here in Charleston. When did you move back?"

He chuckled and said, "Fi, I never left."

"Right, right, right," she said, shaking her head. Her mouth formed a gentle smile. "How's work? Business is going well?"

"Yes, things are going well."

Ransom managed Ransom Commercial Holdings, otherwise recognized as RCH. He assumed control of his father's commercial real estate company after his father's passing several years ago. The company owned buildings across the Southeastern United States. About five years ago, he'd purchased the restaurant they were sitting in. The restaurant was more intimate than large—holding about thirty tables, excluding the private room that could accommodate another twenty if seated—and had an excellent bar. When he acquired it, it had good food, a talented and knowledgeable bar staff, and hit-or-miss service otherwise. More recently, he brought on board a new manager, recruited new servers and head chef, and changed the name to the Crimson Room. Now he had a restaurant with exceptional food, excellent service, and a more impressive staff.

As he and Fiona chatted, the memories overwhelmed Ransom. God, she was still just as beautiful as she had been the first time he saw her on the plane as the United States Olympic Team flew to the first Olympic games that the two of them had participated in. It had been a turbulent flight. Just before departure, Fiona disclosed she had never been on a plane before. He had walked her through the takeoff process and praised her when she maintained her calm as the plane climbed higher into the sky. At the midpoint of the flight and after an especially difficult episode of turbulence, he hadn't managed to grab the air sickness bag out of the seat back in front of him before her previous meal spewed from her mouth directly into his lap.

He recalled her horror and the unexpected surge of tears of what he labeled mortification and fear intertwined. He pressed the button to call the flight attendant. Before he left to change, he asked the flight attendant to bring her a ginger ale to calm her stomach. The long history of dealing with his addiction-riddled parents had taught him much about calming a person's stomach.

Had that truly been over fifteen years ago? Damn, it had. Where had the time gone?

They had met at sixteen and dated until after the second Olympic Games they had taken part in when they were both twenty. He'd considered proposing but didn't, and Fiona had ended the relationship, expressing her need to focus on school, gymnastics, and where she wanted to go beyond both things. They rekindled their romance once more after their third Olympic showing and were together for a little over two years. He proposed that time in front of both their friends and family, and she rejected him. After their fourth and final Olympic showing, they started dating again and he was finally contemplating life beyond the Olympics and swimming. Plus, the added extra weight of overseeing RCH fell onto him. When he proposed that time, she walked out on him with a firm no, and with no other explanation.

Ransom shook the memories from the front of his mind. There was no purpose in going through those times once more at this moment. It wouldn't serve any purpose. He couldn't go back and change anything.

"So, what are you doing with your time now?" he asked.

"Not much. Just work."

"Are you still working with young athletes?"

"Yes," she said. "My last contract was with a group of young athletes in California preparing for regionals."

That was why her freckles stood out, he noticed, as his eyes swiftly moved across her face. The California sun had really brought out the pigmentation. He wondered if it had the same effect on her shoulders. When she pushed the sleeves of her sweater up, he could see it had darkened the freckles on her arms.

"You worked with people competing against each other? I thought you only mentored one student at a time."

Fiona took a small sip of her wine before answering. "Generally, yes, but this was a group who was participating in relay matches together, so I considered it suitable to work with the group. Additionally, it made my fee a tad more affordable."

"Group rate?"

"Something like that," she stated.

For the next two hours, they caught up about work, enjoyed the wine, and shared some appetizers that Ransom had insisted they order. However, it didn't slip Ransom's notice that they shared nothing overly personal—such as current dating status. In one sense, he appreciated it, but on the other hand, he wanted to ask about the absence of an engagement ring on her finger—which he could clearly see wasn't there now that he was just feet from her. That and she used her left hand to lift the wineglass to her lips.

When the plates were empty, along with the bottle of wine, Ransom said, "Thank you for the nice evening, Fiona. It was good to see you and catch up."

"It was. I hope I didn't keep you from anything else you had to do," she said as she scanned the practically empty restaurant. "I didn't realize you still owned this. With the name change, I assumed maybe you had sold it," Fiona said as she rose. "Maybe we can do it again sometime."

"I'd like that. And you didn't take me away from anything. This place runs itself."

"I'm glad to hear that. We can be friends, right?" she asked.

He sensed she surprised herself when she asked because of the slight widening of her eyes.

"Sure, we can," he replied. He vowed he would try but wouldn't promise. Provided that his interaction with her was infrequent, he could be her friend. He would give it a shot.

"Have a good night, Ran," she said and left.

God, he had always loved that she called him Ran. No one else ever had.

Ransom had to escape before the memories overwhelmed him again and he pursued her down the street, requesting to see her sooner rather than later. Instead, he checked in with the staff before he set off to Liaisons to help erase her from his mind. Not that it usually worked.

2

Fiona Campbell departed from the restaurant as swiftly as she could without running away. She had to escape from Ransom. She knew that running into him would be a possibility when she agreed to this contract. But the money had been too tempting to turn down, and it had been a long time since she worked with a gymnast. And she sincerely missed working with gymnasts. The primary focus of her time with the young athletes she worked with was on self-esteem, confidence, and managing the pressure of competing in fiercely competitive sports that lead to national championships, Olympic teams, college scholarships, and potentially professional status if the sport had that designation. While she had a bachelor's degree in sports psychology, her experience as a young athlete and the positive people that had surrounded her during the years that she had competed enhanced her credibility, and frankly, earned her more respect. Over the four Olympic Games she had taken part in, she won twelve gold medals by herself. That remained the highest in the sport by a single athlete, but there were many athletes building a name for themselves and could—and more than likely would—surpass her. And she had no issue with that. She was aware that someone would eventually do it. And if she helped guide that person, she would be even better with it. That was the uncommon aspect of her. Even as an athlete, she was not a fiercely competitive person. Sure, winning gold medals had definitely boosted her self-esteem, but she competed because she loved the sport, not for what it earned her or because she felt the need to be the best.

The previous job forced the need for this contract to replace what she should have had with the group she had just finished working with. Instead of collecting payment from each of the four athletes individually, she collected payment from the group two times her usual fee. The families were from lower to middle-class economic status. She let them make her payments and allowed a longer period than she normally did for the payments, but she had stipulated that she wouldn't begin working with the group until she had at least half of the fee. They saved close to seventy percent by the date the contract began. The remaining balance was owed by the time she stopped working with the kids three months later. And they had followed through by providing it at the midpoint of the contract. Despite that, she had to tap into her savings to cover all the expenses she incurred those three months. But she did it because she didn't want to support only athletes that could afford her fees. She wanted to help athletes, period. That was why she had been incapable of telling the group no.

Her thoughts went back to Ransom. It hadn't shocked her this evening when he folded his six-foot tall body into the booth without being invited. He was just as handsome as she remembered. His medium brown hair, neatly trimmed but somewhat disheveled, caught her attention. It had led her to think someone had just run their fingers through it while kissing him—which she had done countless times. He still wore that five o'clock shadow that reminded her how adeptly he pulled it off. His striking blue eyes were more vivid than his cobalt dress shirt that clung to his shoulders and biceps. And he had done that sexy guy thing of rolling the sleeves up to just below his elbows—which was his habit. My God, he still caused her heart to skip a beat.

It was her luck to see him on her first night back in Charleston. And she would be here six more months. So, it was extremely likely she would run into him more often. However, she made a mental note not to visit the Crimson Room again, or to at least find out if he was there first. The food was as amazing as one of the review sites had reported. He had done well for himself with the endeavor. She remembered when he initially bought the place, but he had never really spent much time there as he was less invested in it then. The last time they were together romantically it had a different name. Right now, she couldn't remember what it had been called.

She reflected on her remark about seeing him again. Why had she mentioned that? She was glad she clarified as friends. They could be just friends, right? After all, they were very familiar with each other. Friendship should be a natural thing between them. Especially during this prolonged stay in Charleston. She envisioned some relaxed evenings spending time together, maybe enjoying dinner, watching television, or a movie.

Instead of fixating on Ransom, she directed her attention to her first meeting with her athlete the next day. She needed to keep her focus on the gymnast. That was why she was in Charleston; not to rekindle things with Ransom. Regardless of how much she might have missed him. And with all the trials the past year and a half had thrown at her, she was no longer the same person she had been when she left here two years ago.

Needless to say, it didn't surprise her when she received a text message from him just before she headed to bed around midnight.

Montgomery Ransom: Dinner? My place? Sunday?

She deliberated. However, she couldn't resist. This was Ransom. Her Ran. The one man she had compared every man she had ever dated to.

Fiona: Sure. What time and what can I bring?

Montgomery Ransom: Just yourself. How about 6:00?

Fiona: See you then.

3

Sunday

"You've made some changes," Fiona observed, her eyes scanning the living space.

"It needed a coat of paint some time ago," Ransom explained as he shut the front door.

"New floors?"

"Kind of," he answered as he moved into the kitchen area. "When I went to replace the carpet, we discovered the hardwoods underneath. I had them restored instead."

"It appears more open," she said.

Ransom heard what she didn't say: it was more open than she remembered.

"I took down a few walls. The house isn't historical, but it is old."

"I remember it being boxy," she said as she nodded. "And lots of little rooms."

"Yes, now, as you can see, it's just one large living space. The bathroom is still in the same place. It's just slightly bigger than before," he said, grabbing the jug of tea from the refrigerator. He integrated the third bedroom into the bathroom and established decent-sized closets for the two remaining bedrooms. They also created a small office, just sizable enough for a desk and printer stand, next to his bedroom.

He neglected to mention that two of the bedrooms were also in the same place. No need to state the obvious or bring up memories of the hours they had spent in his bedroom together.

"I have to add the dressing to the salad, but then we're ready to eat if you want to get your pizza," he said, fighting the memories of them intertwined in the sheets.

"You got pizza?"

"I got your favorite pizza."

"But you can't stand ham and pineapple," she said.

"I assumed you rarely ate pizza, since you didn't eat it that often before. If I recall, it was more of a treat," he said without explaining why he would willingly eat a pizza he used to dislike so much. She didn't need to know that he ordered it when he missed her and that was how he grew to tolerate the combination of salty and sweet. It brought her back to him for just a little while. Despite the fact that it brought forth the agony of their past.

"It was. I have it a bit more regularly now. Well, not how that sounds," she said, drawing nearer to the large island that divided the kitchen from the living space. "Ransom," she whispered. "You don't like ham and pineapple pizza," she repeated.

Ransom felt her gaze on his face. He smiled as he drizzled the dressing over the lettuce, croutons, and thin slices of parmesan cheese. "Somewhere along the way, I grew to like it," he said, not looking at her and concentrating on mixing in the dressing as if ensuring even distribution of it was the most important thing in the world.

When he finished, he avoided her gaze as he moved the salad and two bowls to the table, where he had previously set the plates, forks, and a knife. The knife was for Fiona because she didn't eat pizza with her hands. Instead, she would slice it and eat each piece until she had about a quarter left, then she would pick it up and eat it.

"How are your parents?" he asked. The difference between her parents and his had always fascinated him. Most of his friends growing up had parents with addiction issues, since that was who his parents had spent time with. He had never seen what he would call a 'normal' family until he met Fiona's parents. They were interested in her day, her meets, her life in general. It had opened his eyes to what he realized had been a fairly neglectful childhood for him.

"They're good. How are your sisters?"

"Good."

"Are they still here in Charleston?"

"No, but Mom is," he answered. "What are your parents up to these days?"

If it had been any other woman, Ransom would have missed the flash of profound sadness in her eyes before she answered him. *What did that mean?*

"They're considering retirement. There's a lot of discussion about what they'll do after that."

"Like what?" he asked, wondering why he felt like she was holding something back.

"Travel mostly. There's some talk about getting an RV and traveling around the country while they're still young enough to do so."

"That sounds like something they'd enjoy," he said, remembering how much they had enjoyed traveling around the country to attend her meets. As Fiona was an only child, they had put everything they could into supporting her during the years she had competed. He knew they had also sacrificed a lot during that time. That was the great thing about the internet. He vaguely remembered both of them working remote positions, however he couldn't remember what exactly that had been now.

"Yes. The only travel they did was for me when I was competing. Once I left that world, I think they missed the traveling part of it. How's your mom?"

Ransom could hear the concern in her voice. Fiona knew all about the often strained relationship between him and his only living parent.

"She's alright. She's been volunteering at an outpatient facility for a few months now. She answers their phones and from time to time sits with new patients who are waiting to go to an inpatient facility."

"She hasn't started using again?"

"Not since she began volunteering. Prior to that she slipped and there were a few months where I was really worried. But she pulled herself back in with the help of the counselors at the outpatient facility she volunteers at."

"What about your sisters?"

"Tamara is in Nashville teaching elementary school. She never came back to Charleston when she left for college. She's getting married next year. Cassandra is in Columbia working as an aid to some state senator who's looking at a run for governor or the US Senate."

"Wow. Did she go to college?"

"She did. She has some kind of degree in political science." He smiled and said, "They're doing good, considering everything we grew up with."

"You," Fiona said, "it's because of you they're doing good."

He didn't like to hear that because he had been so self-absorbed in getting out of the situation that he focused little on them and more on swimming and never walking the road his parents had.

"There were others that helped more," he said, remembering some of the coaches he had had that stepped in and acted as surrogate parents for him and later teachers did the same for his sisters. Those people provided them with the same support and stability that had been lacking in their home life.

He was glad when she didn't push that further. Sure, his swimming competitions had opened doors for him, and ultimately for his sisters, in various ways. But his motivation had never been for them, and he felt some guilt about it. He was just glad they had all beaten the statistical odds. The three of them should have been much closer to addiction than they were. But instead of giving in to those behaviors, they used the memories to keep them from walking that road.

He changed the subject. "Why didn't you go into coaching?"

"I'm kind of a coach."

"That's not what I mean, and you know it," he said, becoming increasingly annoyed with her vague answers this evening.

"It wasn't what I wanted. I didn't want to be tied to just coaching and focusing on routines and form. What I do now is more specialized, and I can focus on things other than the physical performance of the athlete. I wanted to give them the support that I had. Many don't have it."

Don't I know it? She knew that he had been one of those who had little support outside of the team and his coach.

Silence stretched as they ate.

Finally, when he could not stand it anymore, he asked, "Have you done anything besides work while you've been here?"

He knew already that she hadn't contacted the friends she had made the last time they had dated, because he would have heard from either those friends or their significant others. That news would have reached him within hours—if not minutes—of it happening. Of course, to his knowledge, she had only been in town a few days.

"I just got back into town the night I came into the restaurant. So, I haven't been here all that long. I've been out to the beach once, but mostly I'm focused on my athlete. If you don't remember, I must go with them to practice, competitions, and meets."

"Even the weekends?"

"At times, yes. I only met with her for the first time yesterday, but my weekends are busy if the competition takes place then. What do you do with yourself these days?"

"Well, I have the restaurant, as you know. Ransom Commercial Holdings basically takes care of itself. While I'm the one in charge, I have some excellent employees who take a large part of that stress off my plate. I check in once a week to see what's happening and take care of anything that I need to. It's a nice arrangement and it lets me focus on the restaurant."

"I meant for fun, Ran. I get the feeling you don't have a lot of downtime."

Lately, he hadn't had a lot of downtime from work besides Liaisons. That was where he spent most of his free time. There was no way he could explain Liaisons. And he absolutely did *not* want to tell Fiona that he spent most of his time away from work in bed with others. Instead, he pushed his plate away after he finished his third piece of pizza.

"I still swim," he said. "Right now, I'm finding my balance. I've had the Crimson Room running as it is for almost two years." He made all the changes with the chef, and name, right after she left him the last time. "It took a lot of work to get it going in the direction I wanted. I made a lot of changes," he lied. It had, in fact, gone smoothly and the employees that remained, along with the new manager and chef, welcomed the changes. What he avoided saying was it took his mind off her leaving him—again.

"So, you swim and work?"

"Yes. I also go to the gym a few days a week and meet up with friends now and then."

"Is it safe to assume you're not seeing anyone? I don't need to worry about a jealous girlfriend arriving while we have a friendly dinner?"

He shook his head. "No, I'm not seeing anyone," he said. Still opting not to bring up Liaisons. Those were not relationships. Besides, they were not talking about having one. No matter how badly his body and memory were providing reasons they should. And before he could stop himself, he asked, "What about you? Do I need to worry about someone pounding on my door soon?"

"No," she softly said, but failed to add any other details. Ransom saw the despair in her eyes and concluded the engagement must have ended badly. He also felt that she hadn't wanted the relationship to end, but it had. He didn't have the courage to ask her what happened with her engagement. He couldn't bear to hear about her with anyone else. He wasn't that big of a person. She had always been his.

"I'm planning to go to trivia tomorrow and catch up with the crew. Wanna come? I know they'd like to see you," he asked, but had no idea where the offer had come from.

Quit lying to yourself. You know you want to spend time with her in any way you can, the devil on his shoulder argued. *But you'd better guard yourself*, the angel on the other shoulder countered.

"Depends on the time, honestly. I have a busy day tomorrow. Speaking of which," she said, pushing her plate away, "I should get going."

"I understand. I have some things to take care of as well," he said, thinking he might head to Liaisons for a little while after she left. Last night had offered no distraction. And he needed a distraction before he gave in to his yearning to lure her back into his life.

She left after they shared an awkward hug. He couldn't remember when they had ever interacted with such unease. Fifteen minutes after she left, he'd changed and was heading out the door.

At Liaisons, he discovered Jeremiah McAllister, better known as Mac, and Steven Cavanaugh sitting side by side at the bar talking.

"Hey," Mac greeted when Ransom took a seat on the stool next to him.

"Anything interesting tonight?" Ransom asked as he nodded in response to Steven's nod.

"It's a pretty quiet evening," Mac said.

"Damn," Ransom said.

"What's wrong?" Steven asked.

"It was quiet last night, too. I need..." he trailed off.

"I get it. I think all three of us need the same thing," Mac agreed.

"What can I get you Mr. Ransom?" Tim, the bartender, interrupted.

"The usual, but make it a double," he said, expressing his desire for vodka on the rocks with a splash of water instead of the just water on the rocks he usually had when at Liaisons. Ransom was not a big drinker because of his family history; but sometimes when he was here, it was hard to decline a drink without someone asking why and he didn't want to explain something so personal to a virtual stranger. "Have we had any response to our offer to buy the club?"

"No, but they have one more day to respond. I have a hunch it will be another no," Mac said.

"Mandy just arrived," Steven said.

The three turned on their stools to gaze at the attractive blonde strolling through the room. Mandy was always up for something. Mandy was responsible for Jon meeting Angie. Several weeks ago, Mandy invited Angie as a guest and that night Angie and Jon had really hit it off—in more ways than one—and began dating. And in Ransom's opinion, it seemed quite serious between them. Of course, there was some suspicion that Mandy was behind the issues Jon and Angie were having. An unknown individual kept leaving them cryptic notes or pictures of the two of them in intimate situations and causing trouble. No one could think of any reason besides outright jealousy on Mandy's part.

"Gentleman," Mandy purred when she approached them. "Just you three tonight?" she asked, with a pout on her full lips.

"Why do you always ask?" Ransom asked.

Mandy said, "Because I could use a four horsemen special."

"Well, you'll have to settle for the three of us, if that is what you have in mind," Ransom said.

Mandy exhaled audibly before she said, "I suppose that will have to do. Are you three up for a slight departure from our usual play?"

"Like what?" Steven asked, his tone wary.

Ransom didn't blame him; he also wanted to know before he committed to anything she suggested. Mandy could be rather inventive and liked to push boundaries, but she always respected when someone said no. It was a club rule.

"Nothing too out there. I was recently thinking about that night that Mac and Ransom started, and Steven watched and then joined in and finished things off. Wondered if you guys might be interested in something along those lines. Except I'd make sure you all got yours too."

"Let us talk," Steven said.

"I'll be over there," she said and pointed to the far side of the bar. "I'll have a drink while I wait for your decision."

When she moved away, Ransom asked, "What do you think she meant about we all got ours? She knows we aren't into each other that way."

"I think she's talking about something I heard she recently did with some other members," Mac said. "She gave one guy head while another fucked her, and some other guy watched. When she finished with the other two, the third and she went at it for a while as the other two watched and then it led to the three doing more like what we usually do. She wore them out."

"Who doesn't she wear out? She's damn near insatiable. How do you feel about doing something like that?" Steven asked. "We've never done that together. We've always just focused on the woman."

"I'm open to it, but I don't know if I'm in for an all-night marathon," Ransom said. He knew Mandy was a poor substitute for who he really craved. Fiona.

"I agree with you," Mac said. "I could use something more than my hand tonight."

"You two start off and I finish?" Steven asked.

Ransom and Mac knew Steven was more voyeuristic. It had never bothered them because once they were engaged with a woman, they forgot someone was watching. Just like they often forgot the others were present when they focused their attention on one woman.

"Let her stew a bit and see what she does," Ransom said, still debating if he had the energy to deal with Mandy.

"I agree. I'm not sure I'm up for her tonight," Steven said.

Half an hour later, the three had finished their drinks while idly chatting about mindless topics and watching Mandy flirt with other members of the club. Ransom noticed she wasn't all that particular about who she flirted with. When another couple entered, Mandy's body language changed completely. She quickly ended her conversation and walked over to where the two stood, surveying the room. After a quick discussion, the couple started towards the door that separated the playrooms from the main lounge area. Mandy shot the three of them a look and waved before disappearing through the door after the couple.

"Looks like she decided for us," Steven said.

"Obviously we weren't that interested," Mac commented. "Otherwise, we would have finished our drinks a little faster and joined her."

"I think she sensed we weren't up for it," Ransom said.

"Yeah, but I could still use something," Mac said.

"Well, it's picked up since we've been sitting here," Steven said. "We'd likely have our choice of interactions, judging by some of the looks the ladies have been tossing in our direction," he said as he smiled at a brunette sitting alone at a table. "Individual play tonight?"

"Individual play," Ransom and Mac said at the same time.

Steven stood and wandered over to the brunette and, after exchanging a few words, he sat down.

"I think I see something that might prove interesting," Mac said and stood. "Catch up with you later."

"Later," Ransom said, watching Mac approach another woman seated in the more shadowy area of the club.

Half an hour later, the other two had gone into the back area of the club about five minutes apart and Ransom still sat at the bar now nursing a glass of water.

He threw back what remained as he stood. "I think that's a night for me. Thanks, Tim," he said, sliding the glass closer to the bartender. "See you next time."

"Have a good evening, Mr. Ransom."

"Please, Tim, just Ransom."

"I can't," he whispered and leaned slightly forward. "The owners like us to address all members by title and last name. They don't want us to get too friendly."

Ransom shook his head but did not argue. He understood boundaries, but that boundary was just a little stiff. His own staff simply called him Ransom.

After returning home, he blew off some energy by doing another set of laps in the pool. Following that, he took a shower and attempted to sleep. Sadly, sleep took hours to come. During that time, he second guessed himself about inviting Fiona to join him and his friends tomorrow night, but he couldn't help it. He had to see her. And if he kept it in the friend zone, maybe, just maybe, he could walk away unscathed this time.

4

"I'm meeting a group of people. Something about trivia?" Fiona asked when a waitress stopped near the entry of the bar and grill.

"They're in the back," the waitress said, nodding toward a hall just ahead and slightly to the left. "Head down that hall. You can't miss the crowd."

"Thanks," Fiona said and walked away.

When she entered the room, someone exclaimed, "There she is!"

Several of Ransom's friends leaped to their feet and moved in her direction. Their response slightly took her aback given the rocky past between her and Ransom. She was also very surprised to find the group was almost entirely male. There was only one other female present and Fiona was pretty sure she had met her the last time she and Ransom were together. At that time, the woman had recently started dating one of Ransom's friends, Jeff. From the rings on her and Jeff's hands, they married sometime after Fiona had left Charleston.

Once the greetings were over, and she sat across from Ransom, she selected a loaded nacho from the plate in the center of the table while Mark, Ransom's friend seated to her right, started filling her in on what she had missed in the friend group since she last left Charleston. The other people at the table interrupted that monologue several times to add information or correct something—including information on the recent nuptials of Jeff. The last interruption came from the person leading the trivia game.

Fiona understood that Ransom's friends were a fiercely competitive group, but the intensity caught her off guard. The seriousness with which they took the game was much greater than she expected for a prize of one hundred dollars. And split between everyone at the table would mean less than twenty a person.

Pierce, occupying the seat to her left, leaned near and murmured in her ear, "If we win, we use the money to cover part of the bill for the night."

"I see," she said and turned to look at him.

"It's good to see you, Fiona," he said with a smile. "Now that you're back in town, maybe we can hang out sometime."

"Sure," Fiona said, feeling that he meant it more like a date than a friendly lunch. From the corner of her eye, she saw Ransom staring at her, his expression hard to interpret. She turned and faced him as she raised one eyebrow in question.

His gaze shifted to Pierce. However, when Ransom spoke, the answer to the trivia question came from his lips instead of something about what she was sure had looked like an intimate exchange between her and Pierce.

Several hours later, their team had won the game, and everyone was tossing additional money on the table to cover what their winnings had not.

"Walk you out?" Pierce asked.

"Sure," she said as she tossed her part on the pile of bills on the table that provided a good tip for the one server that had covered the back room's many tables.

When they walked by Ransom, who was speaking with someone who had been at another table, his arm shot out and his hand seized hers, which naturally halted her movement.

"I'll see you soon," Ransom told the person and then turned to face Fiona. "I'll walk you out."

"It's fine, Pierce said he would," she protested. "Go back and finish your conversation."

The only evidence Fiona had that Ransom was upset was the muscle twitching in his right cheek.

"Fi," Ransom said with clenched teeth, his tone low and almost predatory. She repressed a shiver. And it wasn't a shiver of fear. To her disbelief, it was a shiver of anticipation. Good anticipation. Bad body.

"Ran," she replied in the same low tone, minus the predatory growl. "It's Pierce," she whispered.

"My point," Ransom replied, his lips barely moving.

Fiona glanced over her shoulder to where Pierce had stopped, several feet away, waiting for her. With her free hand, she raised her pointer finger, asking for a moment. Pierce nodded and stepped a few more feet away, giving her and Ransom some privacy.

She returned her gaze back to Ransom. "Don't do this Ransom."

"Don't do what?"

"Cause a scene."

"I'm not causing a scene, Fi. I'd like to hear your explanation as to why you'd date a friend of mine?"

"Who said anything about a date? He's walking me to my car."

29

"He asked to see you."

Fiona hid her surprise that Ransom had heard what Pierce said.

"No, what he said was maybe we could hang out sometime."

"Read between the lines Fiona. I saw how he looked at you."

"What's it matter to you? We aren't together. We're just friends. And if I spend time with Pierce, it will be just as friends. That I promise you, Ran. I wouldn't date a friend of yours."

He scrutinized her for a full minute before he let go of her hand.

"Good night," he said as he turned from her.

"Good night," she echoed as he walked away.

"Everything okay?" Pierce asked as she drew near to him.

She nodded.

They walked in silence outside into the cool of the evening. She turned toward her car and Pierce followed.

When she halted next to the car, he finally spoke. "Do you have plans for tomorrow night?"

"To be honest, during the week isn't good for me. I have some long days."

"What about next weekend, then?"

"I'm sorry, Pierce, but I have to be out of town with my athlete that weekend."

"How about the—"

"Pierce?" she broke in. "Are you asking me out?"

"I'm trying," he said with a half smile on his lips.

"I'm flattered, Pierce, really, I am. But I'm not looking for anything like that right now. I'm recently single," she said, opting for that phrasing instead of attempting to clarify that her fiancé had passed away. And she knew that news would get back to Ransom in the blink of an eye, and she just didn't have the energy to explain it right now. "If you want to try the friend thing, I'm open to that, but I just can't do anything more right now."

"Because of Ransom?"

This time, she smiled a half smile. "Partially."

"Honesty. That's nice for a change," Pierce said. "Well, if you change your mind..."

"I know where to find you if I do, but don't hold your breath."

Pierce reached out and grabbed her door handle. She dug in her purse and pulled out her keys to unlock the door. He opened the door and held it as she climbed in.

"Drive carefully," he said.

"Thanks. You too," she said and waited for him to close the door before she put the key into the ignition to start the car.

5

Ransom waited ten minutes before he left the back room and strode out the front door of the bar and grill. He wanted to avoid running into Fiona and Pierce in the parking lot. He knew he was being irrational. But damn it, Fiona was his. Even if they weren't together. And, yes, he knew she would never date a friend of his. He was somewhat shocked that Pierce consider dating her. *Her.* Pierce knew what she meant to Ransom. It was a line you didn't cross without getting permission first. And Ransom knew he could never give Pierce his blessing on a relationship with her. Now, if Fiona asked him, he would want her to be happy, but the thought of her with someone else—even if it was a friend of his—he just couldn't stomach.

After finding the parking lot empty of Pierce and Fiona, he walked to his car and climbed in. He needed something to distract himself from the idea of her and Pierce. He clutched the steering wheel until his knuckles turned white. Just the idea of them together made him want to rip something apart.

Liaisons, the devil on his shoulder said. *Go to Liaisons. Find someone that reminds you of her. Find a redhead.*

Forget the red hair, the angel on the other shoulder said. *Find Mandy or someone else. It will help separate you from the situation.*

He put the car in gear and drove straight to Liaisons.

He didn't see Mac, Steven, or even Jon—who came in less and less since Angie came into his life. But he caught sight of a redhead who had hair similar to Fiona's.

The woman looked up at him as he approached. Physically, she looked enough like Fiona beyond the hair to fulfill his purpose tonight. He smiled as he came closer to the booth where she sat alone.

"Hello," he said.

"Good evening," she said in a husky voice that had his cock roaring to attention. Her voice was nothing like Fiona's, but that was okay. There wouldn't be a lot of talking.

Yes, she would do, the devil on his shoulder purred. The angel remained silent.

"I'm Ransom."

"I'm Kate."

"Kate, would you have any interest in joining me in a playroom?" he asked. Normally he would chat for a while, but he needed a release more than he needed idle chit chat.

"Which room?"

"Any room you'd like as long as you're open to my fantasy."

"Dress up?"

"No," he said. "My fantasy is to have you every way I possibly can."

"I'm not into bondage," she said.

"Noted."

She stood and started walking to the door that separated the lounge from the playrooms. He watched her walk. The seductive sway of her hips and long legs held his attention, and he imagined several positions with those long legs wrapped around him.

When she stopped walking, he dragged his eyes from her legs up to her face. She was looking over her shoulder at him. "Coming?"

He smiled and took a few quick strides to reach her.

The first available playroom was room four, which would allow him to use the harness if he wanted. He opened the door and held it open as she stepped inside. He walked in behind her before he closed and locked the door.

"My boundary is no kissing on the lips," he murmured in her ear. He smiled at the shiver that ran down her spine. She shifted her weight to press her back against his chest.

"Noted," she said. "Unzip me."

She didn't need to tell him twice. He slid his hands between them and located the zipper on the back of her dress and tugged it slowly down. Once the zipper was open, she turned and seized his t-shirt and yanked it up and off him.

"In order for me to do what you wanted, you need to wear less clothing," she said and let go of her dress, allowing it to drop to the floor before she discarded her bra and finally her underwear.

"Leave the heels on," he said. They were tall, red FMPs. And that was exactly what he wanted to do.

She smiled. "Lose the pants."

He shed the rest of his clothing in seconds.

"Now what? Since you don't kiss, this is going to feel a little different from we go where the moment takes us."

"Oh, no, I kiss, just not on the lips," he said, bending and planting a kiss on her shoulder as he turned her around so her back faced him again. "Watch," he said and indicated the mirror in front of them. Her skin glowed in the soft light from the fixtures across the room near the bed. She had the faintest tan lines. He fleetingly wondered where she had been to get those this time of year. Then he refocused on where he wanted the evening to end. He stood behind her in shadow. The only visible parts of him were his arms and hands. If he leaned forward, he could see his head. "I'll be your phantom lover," he breathed against her ear and smiled the briefest smile at the shiver of awareness that went through her body.

"That was your fantasy?" she asked as she pressed her butt back against his cock.

"No," he groaned at the pleasure the pressure gave him. "But I suspect it was one of yours."

"Mmm," she said, as his hands caressed her. Gliding his hands over her skin, coming closer to her breasts and the valley between her legs several times before she moaned, "Touch me."

"I am," he murmured and gently kissed her neck. She widened her stance to give him better access, putting more of her weight against him when she rested her head on his shoulder. "Keep watching," he said. "Watch me make you come."

He had wanted to do this with Fiona and never had. A small part of him was imagining Fiona in his arms right now, not this stranger.

Her head lifted from his shoulder and through lowered lids he saw the reflection in the mirror of her seeing what he was doing—one hand massaging her breast and nipple, the other hidden between her legs, teasing the sensitive flesh there. And it didn't take long until she shattered, and he caught her before she slid to the floor. Supporting her weight, he moved them to the bed, where he helped her sit down before he moved away to grab a condom and dimmed the lights more. When he came back to bed, she reclined against the pillows. He opened the condom package and rolled on the protective sheath before he knelt on the bed and kissed his way up her legs until he hit the apex of her thighs and touched his tongue against the nub hidden beneath the trimmed hair. Her fingers fisted in his hair as she moaned.

"You like that?" he murmured before he licked up the entire slit and put the slightest bit of pressure with his tongue against the nub again.

"Yes," she moaned and restlessly moved her legs. The quick sight of the red heels prompted him to consider some other positions so he could see her legs in those shoes. But for now, he used his tongue on her until she came again, her hands fisting his hair.

"Now!" she said, still panting heavily. "In me, now."

Ransom surged up, grabbed her hips to tilt them to the right angle, and thrust in.

"Oh, yes," she sighed.

After a few long, hard thrusts, he rolled them until he was on the bottom, and she was on top. "Ride me until I come. I don't care how many times you do but make me come."

She smiled and set a rhythm that had him moaning as he clung to her hips, helping to guide her movement. He could tell she was close again. She closed her eyes, and her hands drifted up to pinch her nipples. He let go of her hips and put his hands over hers to feel what she was doing, then he brushed her hands away and continued the caresses. When she came again, he surged up and sucked one nipple into his mouth as he pinched the other. Her hands held his head as she shouted, "Yes!".

"Oh god," she said as she ground against him.

Holding her tight, he shifted them again until he was on top, his mouth still latched onto one nipple, and he pumped in and out of her. He wasn't the least bit sorry that he hadn't come while she was on top of him. Her body was sensitive, and it was driving him out of his mind. He wanted to know if she could come as many times as Fi could—which one night he had lost track of the number of times that had been.

It wasn't take long before she was begging again. "Please."

He released the nipple and, in a voice dark with passion and need, asked, "Please what?"

"Again, make it happen," she pleaded.

Ransom smiled, shifted his position so her legs were over his shoulders and drove into her. He rode hard and fast, with her soft pants and moans urging him to keep going. And he did until she came again.

"This time it is my turn," he whispered in her ear. He rose, still kneeling between her legs. He lowered them from his shoulders. He rolled her over and shoved a pillow under her hips before he positioned her legs to where the space between them was just enough for his cock to penetrate her. "Keep your legs like that," he said as he slowly slid back into her.

Her reply was only a moaned, "Yes."

Then he concentrated solely on finishing. Her hair seized his gaze. With Kate facing away from him, he could practically imagine she was Fiona. The mental image of Fiona in this position with him had his balls tightening up in anticipation. He fought against the urge to reach out and stroke her hair. He failed and fisted his hand into her silky strands where her head and neck joined. He then pulled up gently toward the crown of her head. Kate groaned, "Yes."

It wouldn't take long for him to come. He knew Kate was close. He playfully teased her nipple as he continued the slow, deep thrusts. She exploded with a scream of pleasure and when her inner walls squeezed him, he roared, "Oh god" as he climaxed.

6

The next two weeks flew by for Fiona. She settled into a routine of daily work with her athlete—some self-esteem exercises, observing the routines the coach had helped her put together, and a little tutoring in a few subjects for school. She also spent some time at the gym Ransom suggested.

There were also evenings with Ransom a few times a week. Because of the memories she had of the time they had spent together at his house, she usually had him come over to her long-term, furnished rental. She hadn't gone to trivia again. One reason was she was busy with her athlete, but the other was she really had no desire to see Pierce again. He had texted a few times since the last time she went, still trying to arrange a time to hang out. She managed to decline without lying. She always said she already had plans for whatever day he mentioned. And it was true whether it was work related or with Ransom.

Ransom had invited her to join him at the restaurant for dinner tonight. It was the first time they had been in public together since the night of trivia. It was a little after eight and was later than usual for her to eat dinner, but Ransom had said things would be quieter at the restaurant if they waited until then. She spotted him as soon as she walked into the restaurant. He was leaning against the bar, smiling down at a rather attractive woman sitting on a barstool.

This was flirtatious Ransom. His smile was a suggestive half smile, a teasing glint in his eyes, and every inch of his body was displaying an interest in the woman as he leaned into her. Fiona felt a sharp stab of jealousy, but she knew she had no reason to be. He wasn't hers anymore, and that had been her decision. Not that he had done anything wrong.

It was her own issue. But boy had she loved when he would look at her the way he was looking at the other woman. She loved flirtatious Ransom.

She averted her gaze and surveyed the almost empty restaurant. She wondered why it was slow tonight.

"Hey, Fi," Ransom called, drawing her attention back to him and the woman. "Julie, this is my friend Fiona. You'll have to excuse me as I promised to have dinner with her. You've got my number. Call me."

Fiona didn't hear what the woman said in response, but the Ransom that approached her and led her to the booth at the window wasn't the same flirtatious man he had been with Julie. He had shifted to friend mode. She hadn't seen the jealous side of him since the trivia night. Of course, since that then, they had only done things just the two of them so there was no reason she would have seen it.

"I could go," Fiona said from where they stood next to the table. "You can continue with Julie."

Ransom studied her with a long look before responding. "No, I agreed to have dinner with you. How was your day?"

Fiona slide into the booth and placed her purse beside her before she answered. "It was a good day. The coach and I made some modifications to my athlete's routine. She seems a lot more confident about it now."

"I didn't realize that was part of what you did," he said as he sat on the opposite bench.

"It's uncommon that I would, but in this instance, she was really having a difficult time with a part of the routine, and you could see that it shook her confidence, which in turn made the rest of the routine awkward."

"I see. Glass of wine?' he asked as he waved at a person out of her line of sight.

"I don't think so. Not tonight."

"Okay," he said. Someone approached the table. Fiona recognized the waitress from the first night she came in. "Tammy, could you bring Fiona a menu, please?"

"Unnecessary," Fiona said. "I already know what I'd like."

After they ordered, Fiona asked, "How was your day?"

"Good. It's been a quiet day for me. A little office work this morning for RCH and then I came here this afternoon to take care of other owner related duties, like payroll and helping the manager with the schedule. I'm glad you could join me for dinner."

Ransom's phone made a noise. "Excuse me," he said as he pulled it out of his pocket. Fiona took a sip of the glass of water the waitress had just returned with.

She watched as Ransom replied to the text, but his expression was hard and unreadable.

"Is everything okay?" she asked.

"Yes and no," he said and paused, clearly searching for the correct words. "An acquaintance's girlfriend is in the hospital. But I also heard that a seller accepted the offer on a business I'm acquiring with some associates."

"Do you need to go?" Fiona asked. "Will the girlfriend be okay?"

"I'm not sure yet. Angie's in surgery."

43

Fiona sensed there was something he was hiding from her, but she didn't pry. At least not here at the restaurant.

"Maybe you should go."

"No. I need to catch up with someone after we finish dinner, though. After that, I'll check back in on Angie."

"How did she get hurt?" Fiona asked.

Ransom paused so long she didn't think he was going to answer her. He eventually said, "Someone shot her."

"Excuse me?" she asked. He had a business associate that was in a situation where someone could get shot? That sounded like a dangerous business. Was that what he was keeping from her? Had Ransom gotten himself entangled in something illegal? That wasn't the Ransom she knew.

"I don't know all the details, but she's currently in surgery," he stated.

Their food arrived then, and they ate while talking about a movie they watched the other night. She explained she found out there was a sequel, and it was currently available on one of the streaming services she subscribed to. They both seemed to rush through their meal, though. Fiona tried to think about anything besides Ransom's friend's girlfriend. When they finished and stood, Fiona said, "Maybe we can watch the second movie tomorrow?"

"Sure," Ransom said.

"What about Julie?" she said in what she hoped was a casual tone.

"Who?"

"The woman you were talking to when I got here?"

"Fi, are you jealous?" he teased.

Fiona felt her cheeks heat, and she turned away from him.

Ransom grasped her shoulders and turned her back around to face him. "Fi, she's a wine distributor. She was trying to lure me away from my current one. I gave her my number to set up a tasting."

"Why did you give her your number? Didn't she have a business card?"

"I accidentally threw it out, and it was the last one she had with her," he said. After a pause while his eyes searched hers, he said, "You are jealous!"

"No," Fiona said, shaking her head, "not jealous per se."

"Per se?"

Fiona debated answering and then eventually said, "I was jealous because of flirtatious Ransom."

He smiled, but there was an underlying sadness to it. "Friends, remember?"

"I know. There's just so much history that sometimes it's hard. Maybe we shouldn't spend so much time together. Let's wait to watch the movie some other time," she said, thinking it might be best to limit how many nights a week they spent together.

"Your call," he said, as if it made no difference to him.

That hurt just a little.

"I'll let you know. You need to go," she said and turned away again.

"Good night, Fi," Ransom called after her.

"Good night," she said with a wave. Without looking back, she walked out into the night.

7

Ransom watched as Fiona walked away. It seemed like that was all he ever did. He needed to silence the part of him that longed for her back in his life. He had her as a friend, and that would have to be enough. He knew he wouldn't be able to handle it if they started things up and she left him again.

His phone pinged, reminding him of the situation with Angie. Pulling it out of his pocket, he read the latest message from Mac.

Jeremiah McAllister: Just left the hospital. Angie's still in surgery. I need to get over to Liaisons. The cops are still there. Can you meet me there?

Ransom: On my way. I'm at CR and can be there in minutes.

Jeremiah McAllister: Ok, be there in ten.

Ransom replied with a thumbs up.

What in the hell had happened at Liaisons tonight?

He reread the first message from Mac.

Jeremiah McAllister: Angie was shot in playroom 4. Too much to text. Let me know when I can fill you in. Owners accepted our offer after the shooting. They want to close in three weeks.

Three weeks was unheard of to purchase something that required not only county paperwork for the property but also a financial audit. He assumed it would cost them a fortune to get the audit done in that time frame.

Ransom debated about texting or calling Jon, but the reality was they weren't that close. Sure, they had the stuff they had done at Liaisons, but it wasn't like they hung out outside of Liaisons. Ransom and Mac did, but that was because of business. Mac was a lawyer and managed various real estate holdings around the world. They often discussed business. Mac had handled the closing on the Crimson Room for Ransom years before. But the relationship with Jon and Steven was different.

"Ransom?"

"Yes," he said, pivoting to face the manager.

"We're almost done for the night."

Ransom glanced at the clock and saw it was nearly ten. Where had the time gone this evening?

"Right, I'm heading out now."

"Thanks. I'll finish up things out here. We should be out of here in thirty minutes."

"Make sure the kitchen is correct. They've been slacking on that lately. I don't want any issues from the health department."

"Already taken care of. I've already dismissed the person who was slacking off."

"Good. I guess we're back to hiring again?"

"Yes, we need two new people for the kitchen."

"Let me know when you set up the interviews. Have a good night," Ransom said and departed through the front door. He turned and locked the door with his key before striding away.

While his car was out back, he didn't know what the parking situation was at Liaisons, so he walked. Sure, he'd have to go back and retrieve his car, but it wasn't that long of a walk.

When he stepped into the lobby of Liaisons, it surprised him he could access the building.

One of the managers was behind the desk, looking a little harassed.

"What happened?" Ransom asked.

"Mr. Ransom. I would have thought you heard. After all, we were just told that you'll be one of the new owners soon."

"I heard there was a shooting, but that was it. I'm surprised there aren't cops out front stopping people from entering."

"They made us lock the door. When they're done interviewing someone, they're allowed to leave. I just hadn't gotten up there to lock the door after the last person left. Needless to say, many members aren't happy about the cops being here. Some were," the manager paused, apparently attempting to locate the right words. "Well, let's just say it was quite embarrassing for a few members when the cops burst through the door to the playroom they occupied."

"Are the owners here?" Ransom asked.

"Yes. They're with the police now. I think the police have completed interviewing all the members."

"Mac is on his way."

"I'm here," Mac said, having entered through the door as Ransom spoke.

"Mr. McAllister, please lock the door behind you?" the manager asked. Ransom couldn't remember his name because he was a very recent new hire.

Mac spun around and flipped the deadbolt.

"Is Steven coming?" Ransom asked.

"No. He left this morning for a book thing. He'll be back in a few days, though."

"How's Angie?"

"She was still in surgery when I left the hospital. Let's go back and see if they'll let us see the room."

As soon as they entered the lounge, Ransom noticed the club's staff seated at the tables. He forgot how many people actually worked a shift. There were always two managers, one bartender, and four people who cleaned the playrooms. Ransom rarely saw those who cleaned the playrooms.

"I wonder if the police have even started on them," Mac said, nodding to the staff. "I'm sure they wanted the members taken care of first and sent on their way."

Ransom said, "Particularly if they discovered those members *in flagrante delicto*. Which I understand some were."

Mac chuckled. "Yeah, they would have wanted those members out of here as fast as possible."

"Excuse me, you two," a uniformed officer called from the back of the room where he stood at the open door that led to the playrooms. "The club is closed. If you've given your statements, you can leave."

"Actually, the current owners accepted our offer to buy this establishment this evening. We want an update on what happened here tonight," Mac said as they approached the officer, in a tone saying he wouldn't accept any argument.

"I don't know. They're meeting with the owners right now," the officer said. Ransom placed him in his early twenties and likely fresh out of the academy.

"It's alright, Dennings. Let them back," a female voice called through the open door.

When Ransom moved through first, he spotted the female detective standing with her hands on her hips in the middle of the hall.

"And you are?" she demanded.

"Montgomery Ransom," he said, offering his hand and plastering a smile on his lips. The smile was genuine. The woman was a redhead and almost as gorgeous as Fi. In the dimly lit hallway, her hair looked darker than Fi's, though.

"Detective Trotter," she said, shaking his hand.

"Can we see the room?" he asked.

"Can you get us some more light in this hallway?"

Mac answered that. "No one told you where the light switches are?"

Ransom turned to face the door behind him that led to the lounge. It was the obvious place to expect to see light switches. There were none. He glanced down the hall to the back exit door. Nothing next to it either.

"Funny thing, that. They tell us there aren't any. These lights are always on, and the bulbs are replaced when they burn out. There are some in that room," she pointed at the doorway where the shooting had taken place. "We were able to adjust them so the room can be seen clearly."

"Then I suppose, no I can't. Jeremiah McAllister," he said, extending his hand.

"Do you really want to see the room? It's not pretty."

Ransom wasn't sure he did, but he and Mac needed to in order to assess the forward progress with the purchase of Liaisons. The extensive cleaning that would need to occur would need to be negotiated in the sale price. Damned if they were going to pay what they offered and then have to overhaul this room to ensure it was sanitary.

He nodded. The detective sighed and handed them a pair of shoe covers and gloves. "Don't touch anything. The scene is already so badly contaminated it won't hurt to let you look. Besides, the security cameras confirm what happened. This is just a formality."

Ransom slid on the shoe covers and then the gloves. He turned and discovered the detective observing him. He smiled. "Lead the way, detective."

However, there was no way he could have prepared himself for what he saw when he crossed the threshold. Blood, and lots of it, formed two puddles that were only six feet apart from each other. From the amount of blood, he seriously wondered how Angie survived.

"The shooter was there," the detective said and pointed to the pool farthest from where they stood. "Angela Bennett was here," she said and pointed to the pool immediately to the left in front of the couch. Ransom didn't know much about blood smears except what he had seen on television or in movies. He had a feeling the smears were from where they tried to stop the flow of blood from Angie. There were no smears of blood in the other pool. No one had tried to stop the other person's bleeding.

"Do we know how the shooter got in?" Mac asked.

"She waltzed in the front door, showed her ID, and signed in as a member here. Apparently, she knew not all the records were electronic, so there was no actual way to check her story. The owners said that there is a logbook of members. And the name she gave matched one of the older membership files in that log. There isn't a picture to compare to, though."

"There is somewhere," Ransom said. "We have to have background checks to be members here. She used her real name?"

"No. We couldn't read the name she wrote on the log, but the manager remembered the name and told us so we can go back and check."

"What was the name?" Mac asked.

The detective studied her notepad before speaking. "Jane Morris."

"Well, you don't get any plainer than that," Ransom said, still surveying the room. "I think I've seen what I need to. Thanks for the information. Once the sale goes through, we'll evaluate the possibility of converting those records into digital form immediately to ensure that we don't encounter such issues again."

Mac nodded in agreement and exited the room ahead of Ransom.

Ransom paused and smiled at the detective—he couldn't stop himself. He was such a sucker for a redhead. Flirting with one was as natural as breathing for him. "Thank you for your time, detective."

This time she smiled back at him, but she didn't speak.

Once they had moved out of her hearing, Mac said, "Quit flirting with the detective, Ransom."

"Why? She's hot. I'm single."

"Besides the woman we were with last night in that room, do you remember the names of the women you've been with here? And don't think we haven't noticed that most of your partners, outside of the ones with the four of us, are redheads."

"Mandy," Ransom said with a slight bite in his tone.

"Besides Mandy," Mac sighed.

Ransom racked his brain. He couldn't remember the name of a single one. So instead of admitting that, he said, "What if she's the one?"

Mac snorted.

"What? Why wouldn't I want to settle down one day?"

"One day," Mac said. "But for some reason, I don't see that day being anytime soon."

"Have you heard from Jon?" Ransom asked, changing the subject because Mac was right. It wouldn't be anytime soon. And if he couldn't have Fiona, he didn't want anyone. Why settle for second best?

"No, but I'll check in with him later and let you know."

8

Fiona had found a comfortable rhythm with her athlete over the last several weeks and had established a schedule that kept her preoccupied so she could only focus on work. There were extra meets and practices that consumed her days and weekends. She had reduced the time she and Ransom spent together, limiting it to just twice since that night at the restaurant. However, that didn't stop her from thinking about him. He filled her thoughts when she wasn't working.

Then last night happened. Last night he had been flirtatious Ransom. It wasn't the first time he flirted with her since she confessed to being jealous of that wine distributor he had been flirting with, but for the most part she had been able to ignore the behaviors and keep him in the friend zone she needed to keep him in.

But last night she had been vulnerable and couldn't resist the desire to flirt back. So, she did. He helped cheer her up after some difficult news somewhat related to her parents.

She had yet to reveal the truth about her parents to him, and a small part of her felt guilty about it. When he asked how her parents were many weeks ago, she told him what their plans had been two years ago. Just after she and Ransom broke up, she spent more time with them than she had previously. Unfortunately, during that period, she witnessed some alarming signs of memory loss—things easily missed in their weekly phone visits when she was living in Charleston and traveling. Because of her concerns and after several consultations with specialists, her parents were both diagnosed with early onset Alzheimer's late last year. What still shocked her was how quickly the disease had advanced since the diagnosis. Before her last contract in

California, she moved them into a memory care facility. And as if that hadn't been hard enough, the lowest blow had been just before she came to Charleston. She had gone to see them and neither recognized her. They didn't even remember each other—at least not the way they were now. They were on opposite sides of the facility because all they did was fight with each other. But both would ask where the other one was. The problem was they remembered the other from ten or more years ago. They couldn't recognize each other now. Except for those rare, good days. And sadly, they never occurred on the same day or at the same time.

The phone call yesterday was about some tests she had had done. She needed to find out if she was going to go down the same road. And the tests confirmed she carried the marker from both sides—double whammy. The doctor was cautiously positive that the results didn't mean it was certain she would develop the disease. But it made it much more likely.

Hence the reason her mood needed cheering and that Ransom had helped. When he hugged her, his hands lingered just a few seconds on her hips as he stepped back. The look on his face told her he longed to do more than hug her. And damn it, she had wanted more than a hug, too. Hell, she wanted more than a simple kiss. She wanted to find oblivion, and she knew she could find it with him in bed. He could make her forget everything for a while. Instead, she told him good night and went to bed alone.

She had a restless night. Her dreams were full of troubled, heart wrenching memories causing her to wake up multiple times during the night. She had been cranky and frustrated most of the day. Unfortunately, she didn't have to work, which would have helped. Instead, she ran errands and found herself snapping at fellow shoppers, cashiers, reckless drivers, and even the squirrel that ran out in front of her car.

Now, she was walking into the backroom at the bar and grill for trivia again for the first time since Pierce had tried to ask her out all those weeks ago. Finally, he'd taken the hint and quit texting her about it. She'd prepared herself to deal with him should he try again. And after today, she hoped she would be able to hold on to her temper if he did press her for a date. However, she hadn't braced herself to cope with Ransom being with another woman. They sat next to each other, his arm stretched along the back of her chair, their heads bowed close as if they were having an intimate conversation.

Fiona recognized the woman. She was the wine distributor from a few weeks back. She caught the briefest glance Ransom shot in her direction before he leaned closer to the woman and either whispered in her ear or kissed it. Fiona couldn't tell because of the angle and the woman's hair.

Well fine. She got the message. Last night's slip, or near slip, was a mistake. He didn't need to tell her this way. She tore her eyes from the couple. Unfortunately, the first person she made eye contact with was Pierce, and they were full of sympathy. He pulled the chair next to him out, and she accepted the invitation, knowing he would ask her out again.

Ransom hardly paid attention to her throughout the evening. While he and the other woman—damn if she could remember her name—participated in the game, they spent most of the time huddled together talking. It gave off an overwhelming sense of intimacy. It made Fiona's heart hurt. Then Ransom's phone rang. He ignored it the first time, but when it immediately rang again, he took the call.

"Can I—" was all he said before the person had evidently interrupted him. Whatever they said bothered him because his spine snapped straight. "I'm on my way."

He excused himself from the table without saying anything beyond, "I have to go."

Fiona felt only a little satisfaction that he said no more to the other woman, either. He just walked away. For the rest of the evening, Fiona wondered what had happened and was able to slip out before Pierce could press her to get together.

————————

Ransom stormed into the Crimson Room's back door and headed to the small room off the back that they used as an office. There he found the manager sitting in the chair, holding her head in her hands.

"What in the hell happened?"

"I don't know. One minute everything was fine and the next, two servers started arguing and then one of them threw punches."

"When did one grab a knife?"

"I don't know," she admitted. "I turned my back to make sure the customers couldn't hear the argument and when I turned around again, the knife was flying through the air."

"Ken threw it?"

"Yes, and I think we're all lucky it only hit Sam in the leg."

Ransom scrubbed a hand down his face. This was the last thing he wanted to hear tonight. "They're both fired. I don't care who started it, I won't have that kind of behavior in my restaurant."

"Got it. Might have to tell Sam tomorrow, though."

"Where's Ken?"

"With the cops in the private room. We tried to clear the customers out, but some refused to go when I asked them to leave. They did when the police did."

He wasn't looking forward to dealing with the police again. The situation with Liaisons was more than enough. It took them a week to release playroom four back to them. Then it had taken until they finalized the purchase of Liaisons late last week to get the room cleaned and put back together. But as the owner of the Crimson Room, only he could deal with the situation between his employees. He was glad this was a little more straightforward than the shooting had been. And someone wasn't on death's door like Angie had been.

After dealing with the cops, firing Ken—who they arrested—Ransom went to Liaisons for a while instead of calling Julie.

Julie. He had invited her to trivia tonight as a buffer between him and Fiona. Last night, he had almost kissed Fiona. This whole friendship thing was becoming a problem. The only way he could keep her in the friend zone was to have someone else in his life. That was why he invited Julie tonight. And from her body language, she wouldn't have needed much encouragement to follow him to his place and see where things went.

The other reason he invited Julie was because Fiona was initially jealous of her. And he liked it. He wanted her to feel what he did every time he saw her talk to another man. Including his friend Pierce.

He shook his head at his own stupidity of enjoying the fact that Fiona was jealous as he walked into Liaisons. He ran into Jon as soon as he stepped into the lounge area.

"Hey. Surprised to see you here. How's Angie?"

"I just came to see how things were going. Angie is fine. She isn't happy about the limited movement of her shoulder. Some friends of hers came by this evening, so I slipped out. I'll head back in about an hour."

Before they could say anything else, Jon's phone rang.

"What's up?"

Ransom couldn't hear the person on the other end, but Jon grabbed his arm and ordered, "Go to seven."

Judging from the tone, Ransom knew something was very wrong. To what degree he didn't realize until he walked through the partially open door of playroom seven to find Steven giving CPR to a woman.

"Here, let me," Ransom said.

Steven moved aside and Ransom took over. He hid his shock at the fact the woman was Mandy.

"What in the hell happened?" Ransom inquired, his attention fixed on counting the compressions and then breathing into Mandy's mouth before he returned to counting as he attempted to keep her blood moving.

Steven was breathing hard. Jon and Mac joined them in the room before he answered.

"I don't know. I went to the bathroom and came back here to get my jacket and found her like this. She was alive when I left."

"Should we lock down the club?" Jon asked.

"We need to call the damn police," Mac said. "Ransom, let me know if you need a break."

"We have to lock it down. Whoever did this might still be here," Steven argued.

"The police will want to talk to everyone here tonight," Jon said. "Just like a few weeks ago."

As the other three argued back and forth, Ransom carried on performing CPR but had a feeling that it was in vain. But he kept it up for close to thirty minutes, ignoring the burn in his arms.

"Ransom, the cops are on their way," Mac said, "along with an ambulance. Want me to take over? You must be exhausted."

Ransom shook his head. "I'll stop when EMS gets here."

Which they did in record time, and for the second time that night, Ransom found himself talking to the police.

When they finally released him from the police station in the very early hours of the morning, he refused to let himself think about Mandy anymore. Yes, he was very sorry she was dead. Why anyone would want to kill her still puzzled him. And why do it at Liaisons? But he couldn't focus on that too much right now. He needed to focus on getting home in one piece. He was exhausted.

Once he was home, he stripped and climbed into bed. He reached for his phone on the nightstand and unlocked it so he could set the alarm clock. He saw a text from Fiona sent several hours ago.

Fiona Campbell: I hope everything is okay. Wondered if we were still on for dinner tomorrow?

Ransom had forgotten all about meeting her for dinner. Honestly, he didn't think he could deal with it. He texted back that he wouldn't be able to meet and asked for a rain check. Then he set the alarm and shut the screen off. Exhaustion overwhelmed him and he drifted off into sleep, where Fiona starred in his dreams.

9

Ransom eyed the blonde across the bar at Liaisons the next evening. He wasn't the least bit upset about Steven taking Nicole off to a playroom. That had been his goal after watching the other man interact with her earlier today. Steven was fighting the attraction. Stupid man. An attraction like that needed to happen. After all, Ransom knew this. He was still resisting the desire for the one woman to hold his heart and soul for over fifteen years.

Fiona. After all these years, he could finally admit to himself that when she tossed her cookies in his lap on the plane was when it happened. He had denied it for years. He hadn't believed in true love. His childhood never offered him any sign of it. His self-absorbed and addiction riddled parents had shut down that idea with their near constant fighting where they would fling insults at each other for a while and then one stormed off and disappeared for a few days. When whoever had left returned, there would be some fighting for another few hours and then they would make up. It seemed like they often forgot they had children during those times. The toughest thing, for Ransom anyway, was they didn't make it to any of his swim meets in high school or college. They hadn't even tried to go to any of the Olympic Games he had competed in. They would been more focused on themselves and whatever alcohol or drug consumed them during that time.

He shook his head. He didn't need to go down that path today.

Instead, his mind conjured up Fiona again. Every memory of his time on the Olympic team had Fiona linked to it. Since her, redheads had always caught his attention. The few real relationships he had been in each time he and Fiona split up had been with redheads. And, as Mac had pointed out, Ransom's individual interactions here at Liaisons were usually with redheads.

Since Fiona's return to town, they both appeared to struggle with the intense attraction that continued to spark between them. They saw each other as her schedule allowed—which he was certain could be more often but she wouldn't let it happen. They primarily got together for dinner and to watch a show on television or a movie. She came into the restaurant sometimes and he usually joined her when she did. He mentally smiled that he knew why she was in the restaurant often. It had nothing to do with him and everything to do with the fact that Fiona had never learned to cook, and she had no interest in it. He wouldn't let himself think about the fact that there were many very fine restaurants in Charleston, and she likely patronized them too. But not once a week like she did the Crimson Room. The other times, one of them would grab something for dinner on the way to her place. He noticed that since that first night he invited her over for dinner, they spent the evenings at her place. She appeared hesitant to come to his. Not that he blamed her. Seeing her in his house evoked a lot of memories for him, and he figured it had the same effect on her. But damn, he wanted her back there.

One night they had been hanging out at her apartment watching a movie and it felt so natural for him to pull her close and hold her as they watched the stupid romantic movie. He hated romance movies. Fiona loved them. He used to tolerate them because she was often in the mood to have sex after watching one, especially if he used some of the cheesy lines from the movie on her.

That night, he stretched his arm out along the back of the couch and was just about to grab her shoulder and pull her in for a kiss when he realized his actions. Instead, he pretended to stretch and then placed his arm along the back of the couch. A friend could do that, right?

Apparently so, because Fiona said nothing, nor did she move closer and she hadn't pulled away either. But damn, it felt so natural to have her sitting next to him.

He shifted his gaze back to the blonde across the room. He smiled. She smiled back. He took that as encouragement and made his way towards her.

When he was a few feet away from her table, he smiled and said, "Good evening."

"Evening," she said in an accent he had difficulty placing. It wasn't northern or southern. It wasn't midwestern either. There was a hint of something possibly foreign, but it wasn't heavily pronounced. It was just a strange combination of several tongues rolled up in that one word.

"Care for some company?" he asked.

"Sure," she said in that strange accent.

As he sat, he said, "You have an interesting accent."

She laughed. "I've lived in a lot of places."

"Are you being deliberately vague?"

"No, it's just easier to explain it that way."

"I'm Ransom," he said.

"Ransom? What an interesting name," she said.

"And yours?" he said without explaining. Besides, did he really need to clarify that it was his last name and not his first? No, there was no reason to do so.

"I'm Lyra," she said.

Ransom attempted to place the enunciation of the name and failed.

"Beautiful name. What's its origin?"

"Are you always this nosy?" she asked.

"Funny, I thought we were just chatting," he said.

"Depending on the language, it could mean many things," she said.

"Have you been a member here long?"

"No, not long," she said, still giving no additional details.

"Well, I hope you have a nice evening," he said, concluding she wasn't worth the effort, and moved to rise from the booth.

"Really?" she asked. "You're going to give up that easily?"

"Lady," he said, leaning over the table and lowering his voice. "If I have to work this hard to engage you in conversation, I can only imagine how hard I would have to work back there to make you come. Don't get me wrong, I like a challenge," he said, "but I sense you're not feeling it despite the way you've watched me tonight."

She let out a throaty chuckle that had his cock stirring. "Don't go. I'm sorry. I'm not used to this scene."

He resumed his seat and looked at her. "What scene are you used to?"

"The other places like this that I've visited have a lot less," she paused and seemed to search for the right word, "conversation."

"I see. And would you share what places those are?"

She thought for a moment. Then she said, "Let's just say I'm used to people being a little more direct in what they want. Not idle conversation."

"I see. Well, here in the South, we tend to talk a little before we go to a back room and screw."

"So, if we sit here and have a little conversation, then we can go do something other than talk?"

"Depends," he smiled.

"On what?"

"How good the idle conversation is," he said and took a small sip from his glass of water.

She laughed again. "Very well."

She seemed to open up a little after that. They talked about some of the other clubs like Liaisons she had visited for close to thirty minutes before Ransom asked, "So, Lyra, do you want to go back in the room with me and a friend? I got the feeling you were interested in more than one of us at that table."

"No. I've heard about the four of you from other members. I want you. I want to take care of you instead of you taking care of me. I think that doesn't happen often for you, does it?"

That stirred something he had repressed for a long time. And she was right. Most of the women here, while pleasant enough bed partners, usually wanted the four of them and they only focused on the woman's needs. He couldn't remember the last time someone focused on him.

"You'd let me tell you what to do?"

"Yes," she purred.

He rose from the table. She did the same. Once in the first available playroom he came to, he opened the door, walked to the couch after passing a nearby cabinet to grab a condom. He opened his fly and pushed his pants and underwear down around his ankles before he sat. "Come here. I want you to ride me until I tell you to stop."

Lyra strode toward him as she slid her dress and bra down, exposing her breasts. When she approached the couch, she hiked the skirt up until the fabric bunched around her waist. She slid her panties down and then kicked them off, all the while still wearing a pair of sexy heels.

When she bent to remove the shoes, he ordered, "Leave them on. You still have your dress on." Then tore open the condom package and rolled the thin sheath on his quickly growing cock.

She straddled him and shoved a breast in his mouth as she sank down so just the tip of his cock nudged inside her. She rose and then slid down another inch and then pulled back up as he sucked her nipple. He knew she needed a little to get her motor running, so to speak. She repeated the process of slowly rising and falling until, at last, she slid all the way down and he groaned as he released her breast. He rested his head back on the back of the couch. "Ride," he ordered in a voice dark with need as his hands roamed over her hips and thighs. Finally, they settled on her hips to help control her rhythm and forced her into a faster ride as he groaned, "Yes."

When he felt her inner muscles clamp and release and then clamp again, he couldn't stop his hips from rising. It felt good to have someone else do the work for his pleasure. Sure, he didn't mind making the women he had sex with feel good, but at times, he wanted to be the one focused on.

Damn Fiona for that. She had always enjoyed making him come.

Driving Fiona from his mind again, he squeezed Lyra's hips more firmly to guide her motion. His hips continued to buck up to meet her. Rather than fixating on Fiona, his attention was solely on the sensation of Lyra's internal muscles clutching him. He shouted his release as his fingers dug into her hips as he held her tight against him, grinding her hips against his.

"Better?" she asked a few minutes later.

"Yes," he said. "You?"

"I didn't finish."

"Is that so?" he asked, moving her off his lap and nudging her onto the couch. "I think turnabout is fair play. Let's make you finish, shall we?"

Lyra moaned. "If you'd like to."

It didn't take long to make her come. However, it shocked Ransom that making her orgasm didn't make him hard again. Normally it would. Ransom rose to his feet as he rolled off the condom. As he pulled his pants back up, he smiled at her. "Better?"

"Yes," she said and extended her hand for him to assist her in standing.

After she was on her feet, he helped her in fix her dress.

"Thanks," she said when her clothing was back in place.

"Thank you," he said and left the room.

10

Fiona kept busy since the last time she was at trivia. And she loved every minute of the schedule that kept her going from sunup to sundown. She needed the emotional escape from the events of the past almost two years. And immersing herself into work helped. She liked the gym Ransom had suggested. She hated the ones where guys thought she was there to get hit on or people were busy taking videos of themselves or others for social media posts. At this gym, it was less likely to be hit on and they had a no cell phone policy, which was even better. She often started and ended her day at the gym. She was in the best shape she had ever been in since she quit competing. The excess pounds she hadn't been able to shed the past year were finally melting off. Her arms and legs showed definition again.

She worked very well with her gymnast and felt pleased with the improvement the girl was making in terms of her confidence and self-esteem. It made Fiona want to consider working with another gymnast when this contract was up. She already had offers sitting in her email. If she remembered correctly, one was another gymnast and was younger than her current teenage athlete. Maybe it could turn into a longer contact and she could settle in one place for more than a few months.

Now it was another Saturday night where she found herself alone because she had backed off on seeing Ransom weekly and she vaguely remembered he had a recurring meeting on Saturday evenings with some business partners. She hadn't wanted to stay home. So, she headed into downtown Charleston and wandered into a bar that seemed relatively tame in terms of the crowd present and had some room at the bar where she could sit.

Naturally, it wasn't long until the single guys started hitting on her. Fiona knew the opposite sex had always found her attractive. She attributed it to her height rather than her looks. She was petite, and it called to the protective instincts in many men. However, the last thing she wanted tonight was to get involved with anyone. She politely declined any offers of another drink or company, finished her glass of wine, and left before any more people could try.

Today should have been her wedding day, and she had to force herself to ignore that fact despite all the calls and text messages that came in throughout the day checking on her. She didn't turn her phone off because that would just cause people to worry. Instead, she mentally pulled up her big girl panties and answered the call or text within a reasonable amount of time. She was only a little upset that neither of her parents called, but then again, they wouldn't because in their minds she was much younger and was likely still with Ransom. The knowledge that she would have been getting married today to someone other than Ransom was lost to them.

As she walked around the crowded streets, she played tourist and paid for one of the ghost tours that were a common tourist attraction in cities like Charleston. She didn't do it for the ghosts, but for the history that came with the stories. If she had not majored in sports psych, she would have majored in history. It was a favorite subject of hers.

As she walked and listened to the guide, she thought she glimpsed Ransom disappear into a building on the next block, but she couldn't be sure. But she knew it wasn't his restaurant. Today wasn't the day to see him. Not that she didn't want to see him. The problem was, she really, *really* wanted to see him. She knew Ransom could take away the hurt and pain. He could make her whole again. And right now, she needed to feel whole again. The problem was opening herself up to potential heartache wasn't an option. Not today.

That was another reason she was glad that Ransom was unavailable tonight. She couldn't be responsible for what she might have done.

Refocusing her attention on the guide, she pushed Ransom and everything else from her mind and pictured the story being told. When the tour was over, she had about a fifteen-minute walk back to where she parked her car. Taking her pepper spray from her purse, she gripped it in one hand and started back in that direction instead of following the group to a local bar.

She reached her car without having to use the pepper spray. Not that she anticipated she would in Charleston. She had spent time in some cities where a single woman walking after dark was like a red flag to a bull, so holding the container had become second nature. She climbed in and locked the doors before returning the container to her purse.

After starting her car, she slapped the radio off. The song that was playing had reminded her of too many emotional things. It caught her so off guard that she hadn't thought about just changing the station. Usually, she enjoyed having music to listen to, but tonight, she couldn't handle it. After a few seconds, she pulled out and drove back to her apartment. Once home, she changed clothes, pulled on something more comfortable than the jeans she had been wearing, and found something to keep her attention on Netflix. She was never big on streaming services until she started traveling regularly. Now she subscribed to several and was glad because she could pick up where she left off no matter where in the country she was. She carried one of the streaming sticks with her so all she had to do was plug it into the TV. She made sure every place she stayed while traveling had a TV that would allow that.

An hour later, she turned off the television and went to bed, ignoring the fact that she still had to spend Sunday alone, but she could go to the gym and maybe head out to the beach. She would not, absolutely would *not*, go find Ransom tomorrow.

Ransom kissed the inside of Lyra's thigh. She was still breathing heavily after he, Maverick, and Mac brought her to orgasm. Being blindfolded was her idea, and he had to admit, he enjoyed the idea that she didn't know who had done what to her.

"Lyra?" he said and then lazily licked between her legs.

"Hmmm?" she asked, bucking her hips slowly.

"You need to decide which one is inside of you before we continue," Mac said as he lightly traced his fingers over her arm and then over her breast.

"Why? Why can't you just trade off?"

"That's not how this works, remember? One person inside for one experience," Maverick said as Ransom slid his tongue back up her slit.

Lyra arched her back on a moan and then asked, "Why?"

"It's not what we do," Ransom said, making eye contact with the other two men who were also shaking their heads, clearly showing they agreed with him. They wouldn't do what she wanted. The years he had taken part in something like this, they had never used a woman like that, even if she wanted it. It wasn't their style. He always felt that using a woman for something like a gang bang was very degrading. Her pleasure was their central focus. If they got theirs—which they usually did—even better. "If you won't choose, then we will, but it will be only one," he said before he licked her again.

"Mmm," she moaned.

"We're going to step away and discuss." He kissed her inner thigh again.

"Don't be too long," she begged, as his fingers danced over the sensitive area between her legs.

"I promise you," Mac said, climbing from the bed, "we won't."

The three withdrew to the other side of the room, where Lyra couldn't hear them.

"She's as insatiable as Mandy was," Mac observed.

"No kidding," Maverick said, rubbing a hand over his neck.

"You have to admit, it was kind of hot that she didn't know who was where," Mac said.

"I agree," Ransom said, "it was definitely something different."

"So, rock-paper-scissors?" Maverick asked.

"Why not," Mac said. "I think all three of us could use the release. We just have to decide who has to use their hand and who doesn't."

"On three," Ransom said, smacking his right fist against his left palm.

"One. Two. Three," Maverick said.

Ransom viewed the hands of the other two who had thrown out rocks. He threw out paper. He won.

Mac and Maverick groaned.

"Don't worry. The night's still young," Ransom said with a chuckle. "I'm sure there's another willing female out there," he said with a tip of his head toward the closed door. "For now, let's finish this."

They returned to the bed in silence. Mac and Maverick traded sides while Ransom stepped to a cabinet to retrieve a condom. Tearing open the package, he removed the thin sheath and slid it on as he walked back to the bed.

Mac and Maverick had started again. Each suckling one of Lyra's breasts, Mac teasing between Lyra's legs with his fingers, and Maverick was stroking his own cock. Yes, that was a part of this a guy had to be okay with—being buck naked around other men who had no interest in being with men sexually.

Ransom climbed back on the bed. When Mac moved his hand from between Lyra's legs and grabbed his own cock, Ransom lifted Lyra's hips and guided himself in. However, a few minutes later, he wished they had put her in the harness. Lyra lying flat on her back with two other people involved in this act was not ideal—the position didn't always make it very pleasurable.

Don't focus on that, he told himself and put his attention to making Lyra come one more time so he could, too.

Five minutes later, she still hadn't come. He made eye contact with Mac, who had let go of his cock and was twirling a finger in the air, silently communicating to flip her over. Ransom agreed. That would make this a little better. He would have preferred her to ride him, but with the other two involved made that position less ideal. He would be on his back on the bed while the other two knelt in front of her and tried to keep their mouths on her tits. Not an easy task when the woman was moving.

He nodded once. Mac tapped Maverick on the shoulder and made the same gesture. The two pulled back, and Ransom pulled out. In one swift move, he flipped Lyra onto her belly and then pulled her up, so she was on her hands and knees before him. Mac and Maverick swiftly shoved a pillow under each side of her chest, laid their heads on them, and returned their attention to her breasts. Ransom held her hips tight and plunged in.

He groaned. That felt better. Her inner walls gripped his erection differently, and it was finally creating some friction.

Lyra moaned, "Yes."

Ransom held her hips firm and for some strange reason his mind wandered to Fiona again. A memory from long ago surfaced. He remembered Fiona blindfolding him once and making him hold on to the headboard. She refused to let him touch her as she took his cock in her mouth. When he had let go of the headboard, she stopped and scolded him. She refused to continue until he grabbed the headboard again. When he did, she continued using her mouth on him until he was begging—yes, begging—her to take him into her body. Then she did. He ripped the blindfold off. He needed to see her. But he immediately put his hands back on the headboard and watched as she used his body to bring herself to orgasm.

Once she finished, he sat up and flipped her over in the same position Lyra was in right now. He put the blindfold on her and then teased her until she was just about to come, and he would stop. Finally, she was the one begging him to let her finish, and he did.

Damn! The memory made him come. He realized he had been imagining Fiona on her hands and knees before him. He pulled out with Lyra still pleading for more and his cock still twitching with his own orgasm.

"Don't stop," she cried.

Ransom shook his head at Mac and Maverick's confused looks as he backed away from the bed. He removed the condom, donned his underwear, grabbed the rest of his clothing, and left the room without another word. He slipped into the bathroom down the hall and finished dressing, not caring what happened now between the other two men and Lyra.

He rarely imagined Fiona when he was with another woman—well, not that often anyway, he amended when the angel on his shoulder protested that he'd done it weeks ago. Most of the times that it had happened was right after they had split. And although he had finished, he remained unsatisfied.

Quit lying to yourself. You imagine her all the time. You need to get over her, the Angel said.

The devil spoke up: *Fi's within arm's reach. You just need to reach out. She's yours. She's always been yours.*

Damn Fiona for reentering his world.

Ransom stalked to the bar.

"Tim, give me a glass of wine."

Tim looked in surprise at Ransom. If Ransom drank while at Liaisons, it was vodka and he never out right asked for it.

"Red or white?"

"I don't care," he growled.

Then he spotted the redhead across the bar. She smiled at him. It wasn't Fiona, but damn, maybe he could find the satisfaction he needed because she looked a lot like Fiona.

He walked up to the woman, who was eyeing him with interest. Now that he thought about it, she looked familiar, but he honestly couldn't place her.

"I'm going to cut straight to the chase," he said. "Wanna join me in the back?"

"Sure, Ransom," she said and slid off the stool.

Ransom failed to pull her name from his memory banks; and her knowing his wasn't that unusual. After all, he had been a member for a while, involved in what had been taking place earlier many times. And people talked within these walls. All members received notification of the change of ownership, and he was one of the new owners of Liaisons. Her not knowing his name would be more unusual. But there was something familiar about her he just couldn't put his finger on.

Ransom threw back the entire glass of white wine like it was good vodka, set the glass on the bar top, and followed the redhead. In the first available playroom, he spun her around, lightly gripping the back of her head by burying a hand in her hair, and passionately kissed her mouth with a hot, needy urgency.

He never kissed anyone on the mouth when he was at Liaisons—it was just too personal. But right now, the fantasy took over again and the woman in his arms was Fiona.

As they kissed, he let go of her head and lovingly caressed her as he leisurely removed her clothes until she stood naked in front of him. The woman started unbuttoning Ransom's shirt and then pushed it off his shoulders. Her hands went to his pants, and she purred when she felt his cock straining against the zipper.

She stroked him through the fabric.

Ransom said, "Take me in your hand." However, he wasn't in the room with this woman. He hadn't even asked her to remind him of her name—and how would one do that anyway? —and frankly, he didn't care. He was with Fiona.

When the woman wrapped her hand around him a few seconds later, he groaned, and his hips instinctively pumped forward. When she dropped to her knees and took him in her mouth, he groaned again. His fingers threaded into her hair and held her head as he gently thrust into her mouth. Suddenly he came so hard he shouted in satisfaction and just barely managed not to cry out Fiona's name.

When she pulled back and he slipped out of her mouth, he looked down at her.

"Thank you for that. Now I owe you something in return," he said.

"What did you have in mind?"

He smiled. "Whatever you'll let me do to you."

She smiled back and Ransom spent the next several hours doing whatever she would let him do until he'd lost track of how many times he made her come before he did for the third time that night.

11

One month later

Fiona barely contained her surprise when she stepped into the entry of the Crimson Room to pick up her to-go order. She certainly hadn't expected to see Ransom at work at seven o'clock on a Saturday. They had hardly seen each other in the past month. Usually, they saw each other at the gym—where he either ignored her or flirted with her—but they hadn't tried to get together since the night he left trivia and had canceled their plans for the next day. She hadn't returned to trivia either. She had grown tired of the mind games and his mood swings.

Ransom smiled at her from where he stood behind the hostess stand.

"Well, hello Fi," he purred.

Damn, when he said her name like that, she wanted to give the man anything and everything. He was back in flirty mode. Just the way he said her name let her know.

"Ransom," she said in a tone that was unexpectedly frosty, given her physical reaction to his tone.

"I wondered if that was your order when I saw your last name on it," he grinned. "Hang on, I'll go grab it from the kitchen. It should be ready."

He was back in just a few short minutes and reached over her shoulder for the door. "Here, I'll walk you out."

"No, I need to pay for it," she said, digging in her purse for her wallet. Mentally, she cursed the wallet case that held her phone somehow always ended up at the very bottom of the large bag she carried. She dug beyond her iPad, the pouch that held emergency feminine products, the pouch that held other emergency products like deodorant, and the various receipts she never got around to logging into her checkbook register.

"Already taken care of it. Come on, let me walk you to your car. I know you didn't get a spot up front. It's busy tonight."

She mentally sighed and followed him back out the door.

"How was your day?" he asked, stepping between her and the street, almost crowding her against the buildings as they walked.

That was when she knew he had seen which direction she had walked from because he didn't ask her which way to go.

"Good. It's been really nice to get back into gymnastics. I'm enjoying it."

"That's good to hear," he said as they walked by a crowd of men who looked like they were having a bachelor party. They called out to her and invited her to join them.

She simply shook her head in denial and waved. That was when Ransom grabbed her hand and held it tight in his.

"Ran, let go," she said and tried to tug her hand from his.

"No, trust me, it's better if they think you're with me. They've been drinking for a while. We politely asked them to leave the restaurant a few hours ago."

"And they went willingly?"

"After I told them I'd cover the tab. They didn't argue."

"Wow, you did?"

"I did. They won't remember it because they certainly didn't recognize me just now. I'm just glad they let it slip that they were staying downtown and weren't driving anywhere. Now, where are you parked?"

"Right up there," she pointed. "The blue Civic."

"That's not your car," he said.

"It's a loaner. My car needed some maintenance. I'll pick it up on Monday."

They walked the rest of the distance in silence. When they approached the car, she unlocked it and reached for the bag that held the meal her meal. He held it out of reach and opened the passenger door to place it on the floorboard.

When he straightened up, he said, "Have dinner with me tomorrow?"

"Why?" she asked. The only reason she asked was because of the hot and cold thing he was doing. Even though part of her wanted things hot instead of cold.

"Because you want to," he smiled. And damn, it was the smile he used to give her just before he kissed her. He leaned in and whispered, "Please, Fi."

"Where?" she asked with a sigh. She was helpless to resist him tonight.

"My place."

"Okay," she whispered, even though she hated the memories that came with going to his house.

"Seven?"

She nodded and tensed up when he leaned in and hugged her. The hug lingered longer than she expected, considering he had been so cold to her this morning.

"See you tomorrow," he said, and touched her nose with his finger before he walked off.

She moved to get in her car when she noticed the driver of another car staring her down. He had his turn signal on and wanted her spot. She waved in apology.

She quickly started her car and drove back to her temporary home, mentally debating about canceling on Ransom tomorrow. She ate her meal and barely focused on the movie she had turned on. Instead, she was thinking about the flirty Ransom that showed up this evening. The ice cold one from the morning had obviously thawed. She wondered which Ransom would greet her tomorrow. She almost wished it was the cold one, despite knowing she preferred the hot one.

———

Ransom did a quick cleaning Sunday afternoon. While he wasn't all that messy, he admitted that he often let things pile up until he felt like dealing with them. After making a quick run to the restaurant to check on how things were going and grabbing a few entrees the chef wanted him to try, he made his way back home. The chef wanted to make some adjustments to the menu and was exploring some new specials. Ransom and the other staff were always trying new things. Ransom had no complaints about it.

He returned home in time to take a quick shower before Fiona arrived. Even though he knew it was going to be painful to see her in his house, he needed to see her. The nights they spent hanging out playing trivia, at her place, the occasional time together at the gym, or the restaurant, were no longer enough.

Liaisons had temporarily closed because of the fire in May that had almost killed Nicole, Steven's girlfriend. Besides, he had to stop imagining himself with Fiona while he was with other women—which he had done another three times before the fire closed the club. It wasn't a healthy thing for him to do.

Since the club was closed, his only sexual relief was his hand and his memories. He had stopped picking up women and taking them home. And he refused to return to that lifestyle. It was why he joined Liaisons in the first place. Of course, he had no plans to sleep with Fiona tonight, but if it happened, he certainly wouldn't complain.

Yeah, he admitted he was a bit of a man whore. He'd had very few romantic relationships in his life. It just wasn't his style. Add to that the fact that no one measured up to Fiona. Why bother with relationships? It was why Liaisons had been such a beautiful fit. The recent issues at the club had certainly caused some problems, though; but he hoped when they reopened, those things would quickly resolve. He was worried about a rumor that there had been a rape at the club. Nothing more had come of it since the fire, but he knew the club was now on the radar of several people they would rather not have the attention of.

Not that Liaisons did anything illegal, but the insinuation of illegal things was definitely bad news. It was probably time for he, Jon, Steven, and Mac to meet again and see if there was anything new in relation to the money stolen from them, a website that implied members had accounts where they could log in, an update on Mandy's murder—along with the hope that the police would clear Steven—and if there was anything more on the fire investigation.

In some ways, he regretted purchasing the club. The club would never make them any money. It had always operated to make enough money to run itself without them having to contribute to keep it going. It wasn't your normal business venture in that way. Recently, they had kicked around some changes that they needed to complete before the club reopened. Yes, it was probably time for another meeting. Especially if they wanted to implement those changes.

They had purchased Liaisons because they were unhappy with how the managers and previous owners were handling things. So, now the headaches were theirs until all four decided to sell or someone wanted out. They had some contingencies in place if one person wanted out, but it was too soon to back out because it was closed. They had to reopen the club or the four of them were out a lot of money, not to mention the refunds to the other members of the club for their monthly fees and their deposits to cover other operating costs. Which were part of the missing funds. Nicole had discovered the money issue when she became their new accountant, after being their old accountant. That made little sense. Whatever. The previous accounting firm assigned her the case, but then let her go after accusing her of stealing the money. Ransom, Jon, Mac, and Steven all knew she hadn't done it. It was just a matter of proving it. However, the four of them agreed she would handle things for them. They trusted her. She was a nice woman. She was also good for Steven.

The ringing of his doorbell jerked him from his thoughts, and he realized the time.

"Hang on!" he hollered as he tugged a shirt over his head, having already yanked on a pair of jeans, and made his way to the front door. He opened it and greeted, "Hello, Fi."

"Hey," she said.

"Come on in. Dinner's getting cold. What would you like to drink?"

"Whatever you're having is fine," she said, walking in and placing her bag on the chair in the living room.

"Water or tea?" he asked. He kept no alcohol in the house, but she already knew that.

"Tea would be great," she said.

"Do I need to dilute your tea?"

She laughed. "No but thank you for asking."

Ransom didn't make his own tea. Hell, he did not even cook either—something else they had in common. The tea he had was from his restaurant. It was a mixture of about two-thirds sweet and one-third unsweet. The way he drank it, he didn't need it to be full octane sweet, but it still tasted good. Especially with the slice of lemon he squeezed into each glass and served with just the right amount of ice.

He carried both glasses to the table set up between the kitchen and the living room, where Fiona stood behind a chair. He deliberately put one down at the chair in front of him and one at the chair in front of her. Which was across from him. He needed the distance from her. He needed to protect himself. They were *not* restarting things. This was nothing more than a friendly dinner. He needed to keep reminding himself she was leaving. So even if he missed her more than a drowning man needed oxygen, he couldn't let her back in again. So instead, he would enjoy the memories and the time with her while she was in town, but he would keep her at arm's length. Nothing more than friendship.

Yeah, right, the devil on his shoulder said.

"What's for dinner tonight? It smells great."

"The chef is trying out some new recipes. So, tonight we're guinea pigs. I hope you don't mind."

"Of course not," she said. "Your chef is amazing. I'll try anything he makes."

"Says the woman who doesn't cook," he teased.

"To the man who doesn't either," she said.

From there, the silence stretched as they sampled the various plates. Their comments about the food and the ringing of her cell phone broke the silence as they finished the final small plate of bourbon glazed salmon.

"Sorry, I'm kind of on-call. I need to check that," she said.

He studied her as she walked to where she left her purse by the door. The gentle sway of her hips, her nicely rounded butt, her ponytail swinging with each step. Damn it! Should he feel a little guilty that he hoped she had to leave? His idea of doing this was a bad one and did nothing but torture him. He moved to clean up the dishes, as she had a conversation with whoever was on the other end of the call. From the little he heard he thought it was her athlete.

He was in the kitchen, loading the plates into the dishwasher when she said, "I need to go, Ransom. I'm sorry. Thank you for dinner."

"Everything okay?"

"No, but I can't talk about it."

He said nothing more but walked her to the door. He didn't try to hug her. He just opened the door, watched her walk through, and then closed it after she climbed into her car and drove away.

"Stupid move, Ransom."

The angel on his shoulder agreed. He changed clothes and dove into the pool to swim away the desire roaring through him.

12

Fiona was weak. She was vulnerable right now. She spent the past three days dealing with her athlete, who had discovered she was pregnant and had no clue how to tell her parents. The girl was seventeen, which wasn't that underage. But she had the world at her fingertips: endorsements, Olympic team potential, and college scholarships.

Today, Fiona had finally gotten the girl to agree to tell her parents and coach. And Fiona had agreed to be there as support. However, the situation would likely end her contract here. The girl wanted to keep the baby. After the conversation with the parents and coach, Fiona left after telling the coach she would be in touch to discuss what to do about the remainder of the contract.

In the two hours since then, Fiona had been aimlessly driving around. It genuinely surprised her to find herself parked in front of Ransom's house. She couldn't make herself go to the door. The last time she had shown up unannounced and went to the door, well, this wasn't the time to remember that.

She looked away and was reaching out to start the car when the front door opened. Ransom stood in the doorway and crossed his arms over his bare chest. He wore a pair of swim trunks, damp hair, and nothing else. He was wet, and he looked so good. Damn it. She shouldn't have come here.

Uncrossing his arms, he changed his focus to something in his hand.

Her phone rang.

She looked down and saw his name on her screen.

She touched the answer button but said nothing.

"You might as well come inside. I know you've been out here for half an hour. My neighbors have been blowing up my phone while I was trying to get my laps in. They want to call the police. They're convinced you're casing my house."

"I shouldn't have bothered you," she said into the phone, but continued to look at him.

"Well, you have. So come inside and we can talk about whatever's on your mind. And I'm not asking Fi," he said as he stared back at her.

She hung up and pulled her keys from the ignition. She gathered her purse and reached for the door handle. However, before she could open it, Ransom was there, and the door opened.

He held it as she climbed out and then shut it behind her.

Using the key fob, she beeped the car locked and followed him across the lawn and into the house.

"I hate to be short, but I have thirty minutes before I need to go to the restaurant and check on things. We have a private party there tonight too, so it's going to be a busy evening. Since you're dressed suitably for that, you can go with me. We can stop at the event, which is for a friend of mine, and then we can get some dinner."

"No, if—"

"Fiona, don't argue with me. Sit down and I'll be back in fifteen minutes. If I return and you're not here, I won't be happy."

She sat.

"Give me your keys," he said, extending his hand.

"You think I'd sneak off while you're in the shower?"

"I wouldn't put it past you to do exactly that," he said, wiggling his fingers. "Hand them over."

"You have some real trust issues, you know that?" she asked and slapped them into his waiting palm.

"I wonder why," he shot back and turned away, leaving her looking at his smooth back as he walked away from her.

For a brief moment, Fiona thought about calling for an Uber or a Lyft and then changed her mind. That would only necessitate her seeing Ransom at some point to get her keys back. So, she stayed and scrolled through social media as she waited for him. She just wanted to distract herself from her own losses. She'd thought getting right back into work would help her deal with them, but she knew better than that.

She never should have taken this contract in Charleston. She wasn't strong enough.

True to his word, exactly fifteen minutes later, Ransom walked back into the living room, dressed in a pair of black pants, a white button-down shirt with the sleeves rolled up to his elbows as usual, and black dress shoes on his feet. He moved to a small console table and picked up his wallet and keys and deposited hers on the top of the table.

"Come on, I'll drive," he said.

"You don't trust me enough to follow you?"

"No, but that's beside the point. You know parking can be difficult around the restaurant, so taking one car is easier. Besides, I have a reserved spot in the back. But there's only one."

She stood and followed him outside. While he locked the door, she continued to his car and waited by the passenger door. It didn't surprise her when he came to that door and opened it for her. Ransom had always been a gentleman that way. After she took her seat, he closed the door and then casually made his way to the other side of the car and got in.

They rode in silence for ten minutes before he said, "You know I can't read minds, right?"

"I know that. I also know that we don't have much longer until we're there. So why start the conversation now? Who are these people having a private event you've basically invited me to?"

"Some," he paused, searching for a word, "friends." Although the way he said it made Fiona think they really weren't friends. "They're recently engaged. Angie got injured a while back, and this party is to celebrate their engagement."

Engagement? Really? Could she not catch a break?

"I see," she said. "Wait. Angie? The one that was shot? I thought that was a business acquaintance."

"Yes, and that's probably a better word. We won't stay long. Long enough for me to make sure things are running smoothly. Their party is more of a drop in event in the private dining room. We rarely do private events, but this was an exception."

"Because they're your friends, or you do business with them?"

Ransom remained silent. When they arrived at the restaurant, he took her straight to the room near the opposite end of the bar from where they usually sat and ate.

"Hey, Jon. Angie," Ransom said. "Congrats again."

"Thanks," Jon said, but he was studying Fiona with a curious gleam in his eye.

"This is Fiona Campbell," Ransom said. "Fiona, this is Jon and Angie, the couple of the hour."

"Nice to meet you," Fiona said, shaking Jon's hand and then Angie's.

"You too," Angie said. Fiona had a feeling the first chance available, Angie would ask about the relationship.

"I'm his—"

"Fiona's an old friend," Ransom interrupted.

Fiona hoped she hid the stab of pain that gave her. He relegated her to an old friend. Well, in a way, that wasn't wrong, but it still hurt because their relationship had been so much more than that. Of course, she was why they were in the friend zone.

Another couple joined them, and Ransom introduced them as Nicole and Steven.

"I need to go check on a few things," Ransom said. "I'm going to leave her with you guys for a few minutes."

And then he was gone. Fiona suffered through the uncomfortable conversation one often had with people you just met. What do you do? Where are you from? How long had she been in Charleston? She was incredibly thankful when Ransom returned.

They stayed a little longer, chatting with various people in the room, before Ransom stated, "We need to leave in order to make our reservations."

"When did you make reservations?"

"I can multitask," he said as they left the room.

They walked in silence a few blocks before he put his hand on her back and turned her into the entry of an Asian-fusion place.

Once seated and they had placed their order, he demanded, "Now tell me what's wrong?"

13

Ransom waited as Fiona seemed to gather her thoughts.

"Just a rough situation with my athlete. I think my contract is going to end sooner than expected."

"And that upset you enough to come sit outside my house for half an hour?"

He was certain there was something she was keeping from him.

"Talk to me, Fi."

"I needed a friend, is all. But, because of privacy stuff, I can't talk about it."

"Bull, Fi. You and I both know you can talk about that stuff. It's not like you're a counselor bound by confidentiality laws."

She leaned in and whispered, "But I can't. Not about this."

He studied her and then raised his hand to get the attention of the waiter.

"Please bring the lady a glass of pinot noir," he said, his eyes fixed firmly on hers.

"Yes sir. Would you care for anything?"

"No, I'm good with water. Thank you."

"Ransom, I don't want any wine," she said.

"Just one glass. It'll relax you."

He pushed because he needed to know what was going on. He sensed she was keeping something from him since she returned to town. He wanted to know what it was and why. And he wanted to know tonight.

"Why would your contract end early? Are they unhappy with your services?" he asked.

"No," she said.

"Then the kid's a brat? You want to end the contract?"

"No," she said. "She's a sweet, good kid."

"Then what the hell, Fiona?" he asked, leaning forward and lowering his voice.

"She's pregnant," she whispered.

Ransom sat back in his chair. "Well, that would certainly affect her training, wouldn't it?"

This time Fiona only nodded.

"And this upsets you because..." he asked.

That question took her a lot longer to answer. "It just does, okay?"

"No. Why does it upset you, Fiona?"

"I needed the job," she said.

Ransom accepted that, especially after what she had shared about her last contract, but he had a feeling it was much more than the money.

Just as he was about to ask about the fiancé rumor he had heard, the waiter reappeared with a glass of wine and some of their selections from the tapas style menu.

Instead of pushing it, they ate in silence. When they finished, he paid, and they walked back to the Crimson Room, and he checked in once more before announcing he was going home.

Maybe she would talk more in the privacy of his home.

When they entered his home, however, Fiona surprised him, but not by going and sitting down on the couch and telling him what the problem was. Instead, she pushed him back against the door he just closed and kissed him.

"Make me forget," she whispered against his lips in between kisses.

Ransom fought the temptation to wrap his arms around her. He couldn't be casual with her. It was all or nothing with her. It always had been and always will be. He couldn't accept what she was offering.

With a firm grip on her shoulders, he pushed her away from him until his arms straightened.

"Fiona, don't," he said.

"Please," she pleaded, "make me forget?"

"Make you forget what? Fi, talk to me," he said, gently shaking her.

"No, damn it," she said, trying to break the hold he had on her shoulders and step back against him.

"No," he said, holding his grip secure.

"Why not?"

"Because I think you need to talk about whatever it is. Not forget. I'll be an ear, but I can't be more than that."

"Please, Ransom?"

"No," he said, and he hadn't faltered, of which he was pretty damn proud. She was begging him. He could see pain in her eyes, and he wanted to take that pain away. God, how he wanted to give in and make her feel better.

Suddenly, his arms fell to his sides as Fiona stepped back. The pain in her eyes was gone, replaced by anger glittering in unshed tears. "You're telling me that if I walked back to your bedroom, stripped, and climbed into your bed, you wouldn't join me?"

"That's what I'm saying," he said, even though it would take a lot of self-control to avoid doing that.

She spun away from him, grabbed her purse from where she dropped it on the floor, and snatched her keys off the table.

"Thanks a lot," she threw over her shoulder and stormed out.

Ransom could only stare at the door as it slammed behind her.

"What in the hell just happened?" he asked the empty room.

He grabbed his phone and called her. Of course, it didn't surprise him when she failed to answer.

He left a voicemail. "Fi, I know you're mad at me; but in the morning you'll be very glad I didn't take you up on that offer. And text me to let me know you get home alright."

Ransom paced, checking his phone every few minutes. Finally, twenty minutes after she left, the text message came in.

Fiona Campbell: Home.

Ransom: Thanks. See you tomorrow.

Her lack of an answer didn't surprise him either.

Fiona felt mortified. She just threw herself at Ransom, begging him to take her to bed. She might have been angry initially, but she was grateful for his resistance.

She almost texted him back to thank him for not taking her up on the offer. Instead, she went through her evening routine of brushing her teeth, washing her face, and after completing the rest of her skin care regime, she crawled into bed.

And there the memories joined her. Memories she wished she could forget. Memories she never wanted to forget. Memories of happy times. Memories of sad times. She knew everything would come to a head soon; and while part of her dreaded it, the other part of her welcomed it. Eventually, she was going to have to tell him everything. And one of two things would happen. He would forgive her, or she would never see him again.

14

Fiona threw the car in park and jumped out in time to see Ransom stalk through the front door of his bungalow and slam it shut behind him. She stormed in seconds later.

"What is wrong with you?" she demanded, charging into his living room and then slamming the door behind her. "You were downright rude to that guy."

"He was hitting on you."

"So what? It isn't like we're together," she said, waving a hand between them. He'd made that crystal clear last night when he turned her down.

When he just stared at her, she asked, "What? Today you want me? Because just last night when I begged you to take me to bed, you turned me down."

He remained silent.

She crossed her arms over her chest and waited. He wanted her or not; but he'd no longer get to play with her one day and ignore her the next.

"Tell me what you want from me, Ransom, because to be honest, I can't do this anymore. One minute you flirt with me. The next you don't. But heaven help me if I'm with another guy. You don't want me, but you don't want anyone else to want me. How is that fair? What do you want from me, Ran?"

"What do I want from you? What do I want from you?" he said, his voice intensifying with each word.

"Yes. I need to understand what you want from me!" she cried, flinging her arms wide.

"I want you, Fi. It's always been you. I've wanted you since you threw up in my lap on the plane when we were sixteen. I've looked for you in every woman I've been with each time you walked away from me. I," he yelled, pointing at his chest, "want you," he finished pointing at her.

Fiona heard the emotion in his voice: longing, desire, and dare she label the last love? There was anger there, too. He held his temper barely in check. Well, that was okay because hers was hanging by a thread too.

"Why did you push me away last night?" she demanded, her hands planted on her hips.

"Because I knew it wasn't what you needed. Because I know you'll walk away from me again. And when you do, you'll leave my heart in a million pieces, like you've done before. You can't take it?" he demanded. "I can't take it, Fi. You've had my heart for over a decade. You swoop in and I hand it over every time. You keep it for a while and then you hand it back to me in pieces."

"You know why I leave? Because I keep wondering when the bubble will burst. Ransom, something always rips the rug out from under me when I find happiness. You can't take it? Well, I can't either. I can't have that happiness ripped away from me one more time. Especially if it was you."

"Fi—"

"No, you don't get to blame all of this on me," she interrupted, finally letting the tears fall from her eyes. "You say you've wanted me since we were sixteen. Well, guess what? I've *loved* you since you asked the flight attendant to bring me a ginger ale. And every time I love someone, they're taken from me. I can't take it if you're taken from me, too."

"Fio—" he said, moving into her personal space.

"Damn it," she interrupted him as she seized a handful of his shirt, pulled him down, and pressed her lips to his.

———————

Ransom stood frozen for the three seconds it took him to comprehend two things. First, Fiona still loved him. Second, she was kissing him like she would never kiss him again. She was going to walk away from him. Again. And this time, he knew if he let her, it would be the last time he would see her. His arms wrapped around her and hauled her tight against him as he tried to deepen the kiss by brushing his tongue against her lips. When hers opened, Ransom backed her up against the wall as his tongue swept into her mouth.

He used the wall and his body to keep her in place. His hands grabbed hers and raised them above her head. He held them there with his right hand. The left glided down her body and dove into the elastic waist of her yoga pants. He silently groaned when he realized she wore no underwear. He pressed his hand into the warm valley between her legs and slid a finger along her damp slit before he inserted it inside her. When Fiona moaned into his mouth, he slid the finger out until it almost left the heated passage and then pushed it back in.

He tore his mouth from her and spread kisses along her cheek until he reached her ear and whispered, "Let go, Fi. After you do, I'll make you come again with my mouth; and after that, I'll make you come with my cock. Let go, Fi. Let me in, Fi. Let me love you, Fi."

With his last words, she shattered and ground against the palm of his hand. As the spasms slowed, Ransom yanked her pants down and before she could stop him, he knelt and brushed his tongue against her center.

"Ran," she whimpered as her hands shifted to his head and her fingers restlessly stroked his scalp as he teased her with his tongue until she exploded again.

Ransom surged to his feet as his hands went to his waistband of his workout shorts. What he denied her last night didn't cross his mind. Tonight, he would have her, even if it was the last time.

"Lose the pants Fi, now," he murmured, stepping close and waiting just long enough for her to free one leg before he grabbed her hips and lifted her. Using the wall to support her, he thrust into her, his hands holding her butt. His lips found hers again, and his tongue mimicked the rhythm of his hips.

Fiona was the one to break the kiss this time and buried her face against his shoulder as she panted.

Ransom felt her inner walls tug at his cock as he moved within her. No one felt like Fiona. It only took another minute for them to reach the peak together, and Fiona bit his shoulder to muffle her cry.

Ransom pushed her against the wall to ease some of the strain on his arms, but he remained buried deep within her. He held her until the blood returned to the rest of his body. Then, instead of lowering her legs, he adjusted his grasp and carried her to the living room where he sat on the couch, still holding her, his cock still held intimately by her body.

"We always had great make up sex," Fiona breathed against his neck.

He laughed softly. "Yeah, we did."

"Let me go," she said.

"No," he said and using one hand to keep her in place, he lifted the other and grabbed her chin and forced her to look at him. "Quit pushing me away, Fi, and I'll quit treating you like I don't desperately want you. Let me in. Nothing is going to take me from you."

"You don't know that," she said, tears filling her eyes again. "Every time—" she halted with a shake of her head.

"Why do you say that, Fiona?"

"Because every guy I've dated besides you has died. My baby died," she sobbed and broke the hold he had on her chin and buried her face in his neck.

Baby? What baby?

"Fi," he said, attempting to push her back so he could look at her face again. She fought him and wrapped her arms tightly around his shoulders and wept against his neck.

"She was so beautiful. So precious, so sweet. She had your eyes. And three months after she was born, she was gone. Her little brain had a very big tumor and there was nothing they could do."

Ransom held her as she cried, but he couldn't quite comprehend what she was telling him. He had a daughter. A daughter he had never met. Fiona had been pregnant and kept it from him?

He had no clue how long he held her as she cried and tried to grasp the fact that he'd been a father. Finally, he noticed that her sobs had subsided.

He lifted her head again. This time, she allowed him without a fight. He met her eyes with his. "You were pregnant?"

He made sure that his tone was soft and low, almost soothing. Inside, he was seething. While he was positive he hadn't been ready to be a father before, and he was fairly certain he wasn't ready now, he would have stepped up to the plate and taken care of her and the baby if that was what she wanted.

"After the last time that we decided to go our separate ways, I started feeling tired all the time I went to the doctor and found out I was about 4 months along. It never dawned on me that my period hadn't come on in those months. It could be irregular after the years of dieting restrictions. I came back to see you and tell you."

"Why didn't you tell me?"

"I saw you with another woman," she said.

"Why did that stop you? The Fiona I remember—"

"You were—what's that saying, balls deep?—in her. You had her bent over the back of this very couch. I didn't think it was the best time to tell you that you were going to be a father."

"You could have called." He felt no guilt over her seeing him with another woman. Fiona had ended their relationship.

"No, I decided that if you'd moved on, so could I."

"Were you ever going to tell me?" Ransom asked. He heard the anger in his voice and tried to control his temper. He needed to or he knew he would say something to hurt her.

"Honestly? I don't know. When she got sick, I considered reaching out to you, but then she was gone within days of them discovering the tumor."

"Where is she?"

"All babies go to heaven," she whispered.

"No, where is she buried?"

"I was living in Georgia at that time."

Georgia. Anywhere in Georgia was a very reasonable drive from Charleston. He could have been there in a matter of hours if she had only called him. "Where in Georgia?"

"Ransom, please, don't—"

"Answer me Fiona," he said in a voice low and menacing. He was losing control of his temper.

"Savannah," she whispered, guilt in her eyes.

"Savannah," he snarled. "Savannah," he shouted, letting his fury loose. "You—" he paused trying to regain control of his temper. "Fiona, you were two hours from me and you—" he abruptly halted and clenched his jaw shut until he thought his teeth would crack.

"I know," she said.

"You know?" he echoed. "You have no idea!" he snapped, lifting her from his lap and dropping her on the couch next to him. He rose and paced the living room, clenching and unclenching his hands with each step. He was still naked from the waist down, but his shirt covered him enough to be decent.

"So," he began, still struggling to gain ahold of his temper. He took several deep breaths through his nose. He turned back to face her. "The last time we were together was, what, two years ago? So, she," he paused once again, breathing deeply several times as he quickly calculated the passage of time, "died about a year ago."

"Eleven months ago."

"Elev—," he said and cut off the word as he clenched his jaw shut.

"Ransom, this wasn't how I wanted you to find out."

"And just exactly when was I going to know Fiona? And what if she hadn't died? Did you ever plan to introduce me to my child?" he asked again and turned to pace away from her. Then he swung back around and asked, "Am I on her birth certificate?"

She nodded.

"Which question are you answering yes to, Fi?"

"Both."

"And just when do you think you would have introduced her to me?"

"I don't know. I was working up the nerve to do so just before she started showing signs that something was wrong. I hadn't even told my parents."

"Your parents don't even know?" he bellowed, letting his temper fly. "Damn it, Fiona. I had the right to know."

"You deserved to know when you'd already moved on and were screwing another woman right here in this room?" she shrieked

"Yes," he fired back.

He paid no attention to the tears streaming down her face again. His temper was so far gone that he couldn't begin to process that she was still grieving her loss. His loss was brand spanking new. Hers was eleven months old. Eleven months!

"I would have been there for you. I would have been there for her," he said as he carried on with his pacing. He swung around again. "What was her name?"

It took her several seconds to answer him. "Savannah Hope."

"Savannah Hope Ransom," he whispered.

She nodded. "I called her Hope."

"You named the baby after my grandmother?"

"Yours and mine," she wept. "I miss my baby girl."

"Well, I never got to meet her," he bitterly remarked and turned away from her, pacing again. "Thanks for that."

"No," she sharply replied, "you don't get to do that to me. I was doing what I thought was best. You were never one to wait around. You always found someone else to warm your bed."

"Because you left me!" he roared. "What? Did you expect me to sit here and wait for the possibility you'd come back to me?"

She cried as he paced for several minutes.

"You said everyone you've been involved with outside of me has died. Just how many have there been Fi?"

She gasped and then fired back, "Not nearly as many as I think you've been with."

"Not fair," he shot back.

"Completely fair. And there have been five. I was even engaged to one."

"And just exactly how did they die?" he asked, processing the fact that she had been engaged like he had heard.

"Two were car accidents, one was some freak accident at work, one in the line of duty, and one in a skydiving accident."

"And which one achieved fiancé status?"

"The skydiving accident," she admitted.

"So, in the fifteen years we've known each other, we dated off and on for close to twelve years of that time. And you've lost five other boyfriends? Maybe you killed them."

"Ran, I know you're hurt and angry, but there is no need to be nasty," she retorted. "You know me better than that."

He chose not to acknowledge what she said, but she had a point. He hadn't been living like a monk, as she said. And he knew there was no way she could have killed her other boyfriends. It wasn't in her. She couldn't even squish a bug.

"Where was the fiancé in all of them?" he asked, even though he already knew. He needed to hear her say it.

"He was after our last split. He was willing to take care of the baby even though it wasn't his, but then she died. He thought it would help me get over losing her. I was with him when he died. His chute didn't open. Mine did."

"When did you get into skydiving?"

"It was something he liked," she said with a shrug of her shoulders. "He was a bit of an adrenaline junkie."

"I guess you resolved the issue with flying since you threw up on me?"

"Ransom, stop," she said and brushed away the tears from her eyes.

Ransom had little sympathy at the moment, even though he knew he should. A rational part of his mind knew that they had led separate lives. Being rational wasn't an option right now. He'd loved her for so long and the idea of her with someone else ripped his heart out.

And then the angel on his shoulder spoke up. *Well, do you think she could stand seeing you with someone else? After all, she saw you screwing another woman in this very room, as she said.*

That's when it struck him, and he spun around. "Just when did this fiancé die?"

"Six months ago."

"Shit," he said and combed his fingers through his hair. She moved back to Charleston almost four months ago.

"I don't know why that bothers you so much," she retorted, getting to her feet.

"You're still grieving him," he said as she picked up his shorts and threw them at him before she adjusted her own pants that still clung to one of her legs and then slipped her bare leg into them and yanked them up.

"I'm grieving for her more," she said.

"So, you don't miss your fiancé? The guy you were going to marry? The guy you loved enough to marry?"

"I do, but..." she trailed off, her eyes boring deep into his. "Why does it bother you so much that I said yes to him?"

"Because you said no to me!" Ransom shouted, pointing at himself. "You said no and walked away from me."

"Rans—"

"No, the first time you walked away, I know it was probably a good thing. We were young and the idea of marrying was something I couldn't wrap my brain around. Then we got back together. I had a ring and everything. And when I got down on my knee, my heart on my sleeve, in a very public proposal, you walked away. Again. When you waltzed back into my life the last time, you turned me down again in my bed. Now I learn during those years we were apart you were involved with other men—"

"Like you haven't slept with other women. At least mine were relationships," she broke in.

"And accepted a marriage proposal from another man while pregnant with my child," he finished in a dangerously low tone, holding her eyes with his.

He had her there. He knew it. She knew it.

"I think it's time I go home," she said.

"That's right. Walk away. That's what you're good at, Fi," he fired at her back. He wouldn't beg her to stay. Never again.

15

"I'm leaving for now. We're just going around in circles and we're not achieving anything except for causing each other pain. So yes, I *am* walking away right now," she said. "I don't want either of us to say something we'll regret, and I think we're both dangerously close to doing it. I'll call you tomorrow," she said and opened the front door and left.

Ransom glared at the door in frustration. This is why he didn't keep alcohol in his home. And damn wanted to drink right now. Instead, he dealt with his issues, feelings, and anger in the pool or at Liaisons. Well, his only option, right now, was the pool. Storming to his bedroom, he undressed before he reached his dresser, where he snatched a pair of swimming trunks from the bottom drawer and kicked it shut. Tugging them on, he stalked through his house to the backyard where he had a decent sized lap pool and dove into the deep end and swam.

As he swam, he mentally blocked the argument with Fiona. He had to, or he'd never calm down. Even though he just had sex, boy could he use another round to ease the tension from his body.

Minutes passed as he swam the length of the pool. When he reached the wall and completed a turn, his feet grazed a smooth leg. Suddenly surfacing, he swiped at the water running down his face and blinked.

Fiona perched on the concrete ledge with her feet in the water. His feet had brushed against her calf.

"You hurt me," she said.

"Yeah, well, you hurt me," he retorted.

"I'm sorry," she whispered.

"Me too," he said and glided through the water to stand in front of her.

"I didn't want to go to bed with matters like they were," she said.

Instead of replying, he picked up one of her feet and began to massage it.

"Say something Ransom. We both essentially admitted we still love each other. I've made mistakes and I don't know how to make up for that, but I'd like to try."

"Fi," he began, still gazing at her foot as his fingers kneaded. What did she mean? Did he want to try again? He knew he wouldn't be able to bear the heartache if things ended again. And actions always spoke louder than words for him. Her actions spoke plenty.

"One reason I'm in Charleston is because I wanted to see you."

"Don't toy with me, Fiona. I can't piece myself back together one more time. I can't," he said, eventually meeting her gaze. "If you were to walk away from me again..." he couldn't voice the words. If she walked away again, he feared it would kill him.

"Ransom, I'm asking if we both still love each other. Can we start over? I can't change what I did in the past."

"Fiona, you just lost your fiancé."

"Something I had to admit to myself after he died was that I never loved him, or any of the others. I've only ever loved you. It was why I agreed to this position in Charleston."

"You'd stay in Charleston?"

"If we decide to give this another try, yes."

Ransom released her foot and lifted the other one and massaged.

"You don't have to answer me tonight, but I'm serious about this. But, if you decide you don't want to do this, you don't get to meddle in my life, Ran."

"What does that mean?" he demanded.

"It means if you don't choose to be with me, you have no say over I might choose to be with."

"So essentially, you love me, and always have and always will, but if I say no, you're still gonna see other people?" he asked, and realized he had applied a little too much pressure when she jerked her foot from his hands.

"Ow," she said. "And yes."

"Sorry," he said in the same tone as her yes—flat and void of emotion. "How can you do that?"

"It would be hard and, in all honesty, likely require me to leave Charleston and never return, even if another consulting contract came along."

Despite Fiona still being clothed, Ransom took a step and pulled her into the pool and into his arms. He ignored her protest about her clothing. "So, help me Fiona," he growled just before he kissed her. The kiss conveyed all the emotions he was unable to express: fear, love, desire, and lingering anger.

When he lifted his head, he commanded, "Look at me, Fiona." When her eyes opened, he continued. "I love you. You're mine. But, so help me, if you walk away from me when I ask you to marry me for the third time, I can't be responsible for what I do."

"I won't," she said.

"What about that fear of losing me?"

"My problem. I have to work through that. I will work through it, Ran. I love you."

He studied her eyes. They conveyed so much more than her words. Sure, he saw love, but he also saw fear. However, mixed in was what he believed was hope.

"Will you stay with me tonight?" he asked.

"Since my clothes are soaking wet, I need to stay long enough to get them dry. Let's start there."

"We're going to start over?" he asked. He needed to hear it. Sure, her saying I love you helped, but damn it, he needed to hear her commit to it.

"Yes, I want to start over."

16

―――

"There's something I need to explain," Ransom said late the next morning as he and Fiona stood in his kitchen drinking coffee and finishing the brunch he had delivered.

His tone set off alarms in Fiona's head.

"One of my business ventures, although it doesn't make me money, is something that's sometimes hard to explain. Will you come with me somewhere? It'll be easier to show you as I explain."

"Okay," she said. "Right now?"

"Yes," he said. "I need to be there shortly."

"Could I go home and change?" she asked. They'd tossed her wet clothes in the washer last night with his swim trunks. He'd moved them into the dryer this morning before he had awakened her with his hands and mouth. The clothes should be almost dry.

"Of course," he said, grinning. "But I do like the way you look in my shirt."

"But not appropriate clothing for being seen in public," Fiona said.

"No, and since there will be some other people there, it's probably better if you're dressed."

Just then, the dryer buzzed, indicating that the cycle had finished.

"Grab the clothes, go home, and change. I'll pick you up in forty-five minutes," he said.

"Okay."

Five minutes later, she was in her car heading to the apartment. If she stayed, she would need to find someplace else. Something more permanent. And it wouldn't be with him right away. To her, starting over meant they had to start over completely. That meant dating. Hell, they'd been kind of doing that the whole time she had been here. But that time wouldn't count. The start over point was last night.

After parking in a spot close to her building, she quickly climbed from the car and rushed inside. While she had showered that morning, she still needed to do more than just change clothes. As she debated about what to wear, she styled her hair and applied her makeup, while wondering what this business venture was that Ransom felt would be better to see as he explained. That just seemed odd.

Exactly forty-five minutes from when she left his house, someone knocked on her door. Running to the door as she tried to insert the post of an earring through the hole in her ear, she called, "Just a minute."

When she opened the door, she discovered Ransom dressed in a light blue polo shirt and a pair of khaki-colored pants. She felt some relief at the casual, lavender colored sundress she had donned. She could wear a pair of sandals instead of flip-flops to make it more business casual to mirror him.

When they were in his car, and making their way downtown, she asked, "So what is this about?"

"Do you remember Jon? You attended his engagement party with me?"

"Yes," she said, wondering what that had to do with it.

"And you met Steven then, too."

"Yes," she said.

"We're partners with another person who wasn't at the party, at least during the time we were there. We own a club," he said, turning into the alley that led behind of a block of buildings.

"A club? What kind of club?" she asked. She knew Ransom was a bit of a party guy, well, in terms of being sociable. But to own a nightclub seemed a little out of his normal business venture. And besides, shouldn't something like that make money?

"Let me show you," he said, bringing the car to a stop. "It's a lot easier that way. The other owners are here too," he said, pointing at three other cars parked in spots that had reserved signs staked in front of each spot. "The club has been closed for about two months because there was a fire and there was a lot of damage. We need to check on a few things before it reopens soon."

"Okay," she said, stretching out each syllable as she unbuckled her seatbelt.

After exiting the car, she met him at a door where he was punching in a code on a keypad. The door unlocked, and he opened it, motioning for her to go in before him.

It was dark, but not dark in terms of her ability to see. There was light, but the walls were a gray color so dark it was just a shade or two away from black. To her left and right were doors that were slightly ajar, and in front of her was a wide hallway with many doors. There was another door at the end of the hallway. Ransom took her hand and led her towards the door at the end of the hallway, and she started counting the doors. That was when Fiona realized that the one place she thought was a door, was in fact, another hallway. There was signage that led her to think the doors in that area were bathrooms. The scent of fresh paint hung heavy in the air.

When they got to the end of the hall, she'd counted to ten. Ten rooms. Why would there be ten rooms back here?

Ransom pushed the door in front of them and pulled her through to an area with a large bar, tables, booths, and people. Two couples and a single man stood examining some papers.

"Hey," the single man said, spotting them.

The other four people turned to look at them and suddenly Fiona felt like she was intruding on what should be a private meeting.

"Ransom," she said, tugging him to a halt. "I shouldn't be here."

"Yes, you should," he said. "This is a matter we need to address if we're to start over."

He resumed walking again, and she followed—he still held her hand—but had to wonder why a business would figure in to whether they started over.

"I think reducing the playrooms was a good idea," Jon said.

"We'll see," Steven said.

"Two of them were rather small, and we tied up one of them as an office and storage. Besides, I checked with the cleaning staff and members rarely used those rooms, so yes, I think it was a good idea," Jon said.

"Are you two still having that disagreement?" Ransom asked.

"I don't think they ever stopped," the single man said.

"Fiona, you've met these four." Ransom indicated Jon, Angie, Steven, and Nicole with a wave of his hand. "This is Mac."

"Fiona." Mac acknowledged with a nod and then shot a sharp glance at Ransom.

"Nice to see you again," Angie said.

"Good to see you again," Fiona said. "I'm not sure I understand what's going on here."

That caused Nicole to laugh. "For some reason, they seem to enjoy doing that to people."

"Hi Nicole," Fiona greeted before she shot a puzzled look at Ransom again.

"This is a club called Liaisons. The four of us," he said with a gesture to the men, "own it."

"You said something about that earlier. But I don't understand what kind of club it is."

"It's a private sex club," Ransom said.

A private— "What?" she asked.

"I had the same reaction," Nicole said, "and they let me think something else went on here for a good half an hour. Don't think the worst."

"Let's look at the changes here at the front, and then I'll explain a little more. Just listen," Ransom said.

"Let's start in the front and work our way back," Mac suggested. "This is really more of a last walk through and to sign off on things for the contractor."

The group moved to an open door that let a lot of light into the dim space.

When she stepped through, she saw large windows draped in a dark, sheer fabric. "The new drapes arrive today, so the staff can put them up to give some privacy in here again, especially at night."

She wasn't entirely sure which of the men had spoken, and she didn't look around to find out. Instead, she studied the built-ins that were for some type of storage and the large desk that took up most of the space. On the desk sat four monitors. Two of the monitors, she realized, showed a range of camera angles. The other two monitors were dark.

"And the lock boxes?" Ransom asked.

Lock boxes?

"Also arrived today."

"That was cutting it a little close," Ransom said. "Considering how many there are and would need programming."

"We would have dealt with it."

"The cameras are already running and recording. The loop is a little longer than before, at least in the common areas. We'll download the footage from the cameras in the playrooms and store it indefinitely."

"Still only accessible from that computer?" Ransom clarified as he pointed at one of the dark monitors.

"That and only from my log in at RLS," Jon said.

"How often?"

"I linked it to the door locks. So, when members are ready to leave the room and flip open the lock, it'll automatically dump what it has from the last time it did it—which would be from the last time it was unlocked. If that room remains unused for several hours, it'll dump the footage at midnight. It will be date and time stamped by room. Each room has its own DVR now. This way, we can avoid viewing every playroom on a specific date if there is a report of misconduct."

"What?" Fiona asked.

"Hang on," Ransom whispered.

Why did they have the need for such a high level of security at a club? And private rooms with recording devices? What were they recording? Why were they recording?

"Let's look at the kitchen next."

Fiona turned when Ransom did because he still held her hand and they exited what she labeled as a lobby of sorts.

"We resized the room to make space for the new kitchen," Jon said, gesturing to the bar and tables.

There was a door a few feet away that was a swinging door instead of one that required a handle to use.

Once she walked through it, she could see everything she assumed one required in a professional kitchen.

"The plan is still a limited menu, correct?" Steven asked as he looked at Ransom.

"Yes. The chef can have as much creative control as he wants, but there won't be more than three appetizers, three meals, or three desserts at a time. Of course, the three meals would vary by the time of day as well. He was talking about a rotating menu based on what he could get his hands on. He wanted to use as much as he could from local sources."

By the time of day?

"He signed the paperwork?" Jon asked.

"He did. I dropped it off two days ago. Left it with Maverick."

"Perfect. I haven't been back in the office since I came back to town," Jon said. "What about a second chef? He can't work twenty-four-seven."

"He's interviewing now. He suggested three more to give each at least one day off a week. It would be better if we could give them two days off like the cleaning staff and managers have."

"I'd rather start with three chefs first. They can work twelve-hour shifts like the cleaning staff and managers and still have two days off a week. We can chat in more detail if we see the necessity based on the demand. If it isn't necessary, I don't want to be the one to let four people, and I'm sure some servers, go. Has he even thought about servers?" Mac said.

"Limited. One per shift right now," Ransom replied.

"The kitchen is new?" Fiona asked.

"It is," Ransom nodded as he studied the stainless-steel work area and professional grade appliances.

"Where are the managers?" Ransom asked.

"They're checking the playrooms with the cleaning staff. I thought they could assist with that, and we just needed to do a quick glance at each one," Mac said. "If not, we'd be here all day, and I have a dinner meeting I can't miss."

Playrooms?

"Let's inspect the bar next," Mac said.

Fiona refused to follow Ransom blindly when he turned to leave the room.

"Ran?"

He stopped when she dug in her heels.

"What is this place?"

"I told you. It's a private sex club."

"Why do you own a sex club?"

"I'll explain more later, okay? Let's finish this first."

"Ransom, I'm not into group stuff," she said, thinking that was why she was here.

He laughed. "I know that, Fi. And that's not what this is about. At least not if you and I are together."

"Excuse me?" she asked. *Ransom was into group sex? Since when?*

"We'll talk. I promise."

Fiona barely listened anymore as they proceeded through the bar area. They tastefully decorated the lounge in dark gray, burgundy, and light gray. The lighting cast a muted and intimate glow. The setting encouraged hushed conversations in the booths.

Ten minutes later, they moved back through the door that led to the hall with all the doors.

The doors must be the playrooms.

"Why don't we each take two rooms and whoever finishes first can take care of the remaining ones?" Mac proposed.

"Good idea," Ransom agreed. "We'll take rooms one and two."

"If the others have finished with the room, there's a piece of paper on the bed. You'll need to sign off on any empty blanks. If there are questions or concerns, the four of us talk," Mac called after him.

Ransom simply waved his free hand in acknowledgement.

He pulled Fiona with him into room one. It was one of the tamer rooms in terms of the equipment present. In room one, they arranged a typical bedroom with a small seating area, including a loveseat and armchair. The toys typically used in this room hid in bureaus and chests. It also had one very large walk-in closet with costumes.

He strode to the bed, still pulling Fiona along behind him, and reached for the paper. Before he could grab it, she swiped it up and read. He watched her eyes widen.

Then her gaze shot to his. "A dress up room?"

He smiled wolfishly at her. "Wanna play?" he asked in the voice that he deliberately made lower and added a seductive note to it.

Her eyes dilated.

He mentally chuckled. *Yeah, she did.*

"What's your fantasy, Fi?" he asked, moving one step closer so his lips brushed her ear as he spoke. "Tell me yours and I'll tell you mine," he teased.

"Uh...um...," she stuttered, and the paper drifted from her fingers to the floor.

He kept his lips close to her ear. "Each room is a little different. This one is more for those that like to role play. Wanna see?"

"Uh...um...," she stuttered again but a slight blush stained her cheeks.

She did. He grinned. He never expected that.

He lightly tugged, so she followed him to the closet doors. Without letting go of her hand, because part of him still expected her to run, Ransom opened one of the double doors and then the other. Once he stepped in, the lights, activated by a concealed motion sensor, turned on. Closet organizers covered the entire space, resulting in a giant U-shape creating a customized combination of hanging and folding storage.

"Holy cow," Fiona softly exclaimed.

"Leaves a lot to the imagination, doesn't it?" he asked.

"Yeah," she admitted.

He quickly scanned the contents and deemed the inventory as complete as they could predict. When they first started talking about restocking the inventories of each room, there were a lot of questions. Over time, they found some invoices showing certain stock ordered for the playrooms and worked off them as best as they could. A month into the renovation, they sent a survey out to the members of the club to help fill in the blanks. He typically didn't use this room. The one time he remembered using it, he had asked the woman he was with to wear one of the red wigs. That was part of this room's purpose. He wasn't proud of that time because he'd imagined he was with Fiona at that time. It was after the second time they split up. He couldn't remember the other woman's name and didn't care. That night he had needed Fiona and had gotten her through fantasizing.

He closed the doors and returned to the bed and scooped up the paper from the floor. He needed to double check specifics in terms of the structure of the room. The managers and cleaning staff had completed the other inventory items.

He felt Fiona's tug her hand from his and he let her go. He watched her from the corner of his eye as she tentatively walked to one bureau and opened it. At her soft gasp, he shifted his gaze to see what was particular to that one—several types of toys were present.

He chuckled softly as he strolled to her side while he scanned the walls for any spots that needed touch up.

Once at her side, he said, "Yes, there are toys in here too. Some people like them with the costumes."

He tried, very hard, not to laugh out loud at the look on her face as she studied some of the various sexual toys stored in the bureau. It was incredibly tame compared to some of the other rooms.

She closed the door and reached for the top drawer of a chest.

He couldn't remember what was in that one.

This time, he laughed at the look on her face. That drawer held various types of lubricants and condoms.

She shut the drawer with a loud bang and turned to him.

"Do hookers work here? Are you a pimp?"

"No," he said with a laugh. "Everything here is legal. Liaisons is a private club where people can come and do things they are unable to do in their own home. Could you try explaining a room like this to someone when you have company over and are giving them a tour of your home?"

"I see," she said. "And all the rooms are different?"

"Yes. We have a lot of different members."

"And they record the things that happen in these rooms?" she asked in a whisper. "Why? Is it so others can watch?"

"No. The recordings in the playrooms are only available to the four owners, and we'll only access them if someone makes an accusation."

"What kind of accusation?"

He quickly explained about respecting people's limits and when someone said stop, the member had to stop.

"You remember those *Fifty Shades* movies you forced me to watch a few years back?" When she nodded, he continued, "You remember their discussion on safe words?" He paused again and waited for her to nod. When she did, he explained, "Stop is a universal safe word here. Stop means stop. If someone says that a member didn't follow the rules while in these rooms, we can replay the footage and see what happened. If it becomes necessary, we can give it to the authorities or lawyers. But we don't look at it unless someone reports something."

"They record sound," she whispered, looking up at the ceiling.

He chuckled as he answered, "Of course they do. How else would we be able to prove someone told someone to stop? And the cameras aren't obvious, Fi. At least not anymore. They're carefully hidden to keep people from tampering with them."

He didn't explain that Jon had done that on purpose this time. Jon had suspicions about the deliberate disabling of the camera in the room where Mandy was murdered.

"What if people want to record themselves, you know, to watch it back later?"

"Each room has a separate camera that they can do that with. It's much like the old school camcorders, but there are various methods to transfer the video from it," he answered, wondering if that was her fantasy. He admitted he could get behind that. Some of his best memories were of them in bed. Why not have it recorded instead of just in his memory banks?

"When did you get involved here?"

Ransom debated about lying and telling her it was only recently but went with the truth instead—lies were too much to keep up with. "It's been several years. When you and I got back together the last time, I deactivated my membership. When we split up, I reactivated it."

"And how many partners have you had here?"

"I can't answer that honestly, Fiona."

"Would you deactivate your membership again if we're together?"

"I would, but if it was something you were interested in, we could remain members. But we don't have to talk about that right now. Let me finish checking things here and we'll go across the hall to room two."

He quickly scanned the room for the things not checked off and then, after Fiona handed him a pen from her purse, marked the missing things as complete.

Her reaction to room two would likely be more subdued. It was a room built for sex on things other than a bed—and there were two rooms like that. They were two of the more frequently used rooms. It had an enormous bed like all the rooms did, but it had reinforced shelving built into the walls to set a woman on or to hold on to. Along with various pieces of furniture, like the large desk, set around the room for the same purpose. It had a living room area and one hell of a shower with lots of different handholds for countless different positions. It was a room he had used many times.

It was a room he would love to have her in because of her flexibility. Thinking of her in the shower of this room made him hard.

Fiona stopped asking questions while he inspected the room. Reviewing the sheet, he saw the managers and staff had already inspected the other toys in the room and signed off. He quickly signed off on the checklist and placed it back on the bed.

In the hall, he called out and asked, "What's left?"

"Four and ten," Mac shouted from somewhere up the hall.

Two rooms with the most things to check. Ransom really didn't want to take Fiona into room four yet. Four was the room best set up for group sex and one room he spent most of his time in when he was at Liaisons.

But it was closer than ten. And room ten was a room he definitely would not take her into. Room ten was the BDSM room, and one he preferred not to use. It wasn't really his thing. There were several rooms where one could tie or bind someone up. It was the other things in room ten that did nothing for him—the floggers, whips, etc...

"We'll take four," Ransom said. "Someone else do ten."

He didn't miss Fiona's reaction to the harness hanging from the steel bar. It was his favorite part of the room and a very hard thing to miss. The bed in this room was different, too. It was the one bed in the club on a raised platform. The sides of the bed had steps that a person could pull out to adjust their height while participating in the play, with or without the harness.

He closed the door behind them. He probably shouldn't have, but he was going to tell her a few things that he did not want overheard and felt it was appropriate to do it in the room.

"This is the room I have used the most," he whispered.

"What is it?"

"It's a room where over two people can take part. Mac, Jon, Steven, and I used to be with one woman in this room. And before you go thinking the worst of all of us, it was all about her pleasure; not ours. Jon stopped participating when he met Angie," he said. Ransom wasn't sure if he wanted to say that he'd been with Angie during one of those times. But he decided against it because he was pretty sure Steven had yet to tell Nicole about it either. Ransom could tell Fiona later if he felt it was necessary.

"Steven still does?"

"No, he quit when he and Nicole got serious."

"Were you with her?"

"No. As far as I know, Steven and Nicole haven't engaged in anything like that."

She turned away and walked to the bed. "How does it work?"

"That's hard for me to explain without being very graphic. But the harness supports the woman and suspends her over the bed where three people can engage with her, and one person can be inside."

He stepped behind her and wrapped his arms around her waist. "And I have used the harness without the others and just one woman. It makes some positions easier. I'd love to show you sometime," he whispered in her ear.

"I'll think about it," she whispered back. Ransom could hear the curiosity and even desire in her voice.

"This room may take a little longer to check," he said, letting her go and reaching for the paper.

"Why?"

"I need to double-check the installation of the harness and that they properly attached the bar to the walls. Plus, it looks like the managers haven't finished the inventory here yet, so that will take a little more time."

"Can I help?"

"You want to check and make sure some of the toys are correct? Do you know what this is?" he asked, pointing to a specific type of vibrator.

She blushed. "No, but with a name like that, I think I could figure it out pretty quick." Then she added, curiosity clear in her voice, "You know what that is?"

"Yes," he said. "Why don't you check the linens instead?" he said, pointing to the top of the list.

17

―――

Fiona reviewed the menu the hostess handed her once she sat at the table in the Crimson Room. Ransom was checking in with the kitchen staff and his manager, but she knew he wouldn't be long. She had questions. A lot of them.

Liaisons intrigued her and scared her at the same time. How had he even gotten involved with a place like that? Was the woman she saw him with years ago also a member? Why would he want to keep going if they were in a relationship again? Did she want to go there with him? Did she want to go without him? How did he come to be an owner? She didn't believe that he hadn't been an owner the last time they dated. But she couldn't be certain about that.

"You know, you're thinking so hard, steam is coming out of your ears," Ransom whispered in her ear.

She jumped.

She heard his soft laugh.

"Sorry. I didn't mean to scare you," he said against her ear. She felt his lips move with each word. Then he pressed a soft kiss on her cheek.

He moved from behind her and lowered himself into the chair across from her. He'd had them seated at a relatively private table away from most of the other diners.

"Is everything okay in the kitchen?"

"Of course. I'm just a little later than usual checking on things this evening."

"It's busy in here tonight," she said, returning her attention and focus to the menu. Her questions could wait. Her stomach was more demanding than her curiosity at the moment. They hadn't eaten since breakfast. Granted, that was close to eleven, but still. It was after seven now.

"The special tonight is tuna. The chef scored a bargain on some nice tuna steaks."

"That sounds good. How did he prepare it?"

"I'll let the server tell you. It's a little game I like to play to keep them on their toes," he explained.

"I imagine serving the boss is a little intimidating," she said, watching as the woman who waited on her the first night approached the table.

"Tammy, explain the special tonight to Fiona," Ransom said.

Tammy explained, and Fiona only half listened to the preparation and the sides that accompanied it. She had already decided to try it. She'd gone through almost everything on the menu and wanted something new.

"I'll have that," Fiona said, passing the menu.

"I will too," Ransom said. "Add a side Caesar salad with mine though."

"Very good," Tammy said. "Any interest in an appetizer? And what about drinks?"

"I'll have water for now," Fiona said, "but I'd like a glass of wine with the meal. Is there a recommendation for that as well?"

Ransom replied instead of Tammy. "Bring us a bottle of the semillon."

"That's the chef's recommendation," Tammy nodded. "No appetizer for you two?"

Ransom raised an eyebrow in question as well. "We haven't eaten since this morning. Are you hungry?"

"I'll have a side Caesar salad as well."

"Very good. I'll be right back with the drinks, and the salads will come out shortly."

When they were alone, Ransom spoke. "I realize you have questions."

"Many," she admitted. "Why did you join a place like that? And why are you just now telling me about it? You said nothing about it when we got back together last time."

"I'll answer the second question first. I'm telling you now because I'm an owner, as I said earlier. Before, I was just a member. I didn't see it as something to mention since it didn't figure in our relationship."

Fiona interrupted him. "If you didn't see us going then, why do you see us going now?"

"Because I'm an owner. The four of us have a lot to deal with before it reopens next week. I didn't want to explain it then. I want all our cards on the table, Fi."

"Okay, so what's the answer to my first question?"

"I wasn't interested in dating after we split up the third time. I wasn't in a good place if you want the truth. I offered you everything, and you walked away. One evening, Mac came in here and sat at the bar. It was a slow night and he and I got to talking because our bartender was out sick. I was covering the bar. The conversation doesn't matter, but he invited me to go with him."

"Was he hitting on you?"

"No," Ransom said with a laugh. "The club advertising is by word of mouth only. It's truly private. You couldn't just walk in and have access for the evening. A member must sign you in. But I'd rather not get into all of that now. We can talk about that process later. I went with him and let's just say, it impressed me that there was some place where I could get sexual release without the complication of dating or even dealing with the bar scene."

"When did you start doing the," she paused and looked around. She leaned closer and whispered, "The group thing?"

"It wasn't until after the third time we ended things. By then, Jon and Steven were members. The four of us, meaning the two of them, myself and Mac, had hung out some at the club. One night we were talking with a woman who said her fantasy had always been to be with more than one guy. We set some ground rules, and the rest was history, as they say."

"When you do that, you and the guys do things to each other?"

"No. We really just focus on her. Sometimes two or three would start and the fourth would join later," he said, shifting in his chair.

Fiona wondered if the movement was out of guilt or that he was getting turned on.

"Can we talk about that part later? This isn't where I'd like to discuss it," he said.

"Okay. How did you become an owner?"

"The closing happened not long after you arrived back in town. We'd been talking about it for a few months before that. We had several reasons, but it boiled down to we weren't happy with how the owners and managers they had in place handled certain things. We approached the owners and after some negotiations and the shooting, they finally agreed to sell."

"What shooting?"

"Angie's. Again, I can tell you more about that later, okay?" he said.

"Someone shot Angie there?"

He nodded but gave her a look that said *later*.

"Would you sell out to the others if I said I didn't want that to be a part of our lives?"

"If it was that important to you, yes. The agreement is they purchase my share, or I bring someone to the table that they agree on, and that person acquires my share."

"I see," she said. And she did. However, she didn't miss that he would only do it if it was that important to her. "Would you ever leave if things didn't go anywhere with us?"

"At some point, maybe. That hasn't come up though," he said. "Wait until Tammy delivers the drinks to continue," he whispered.

Now Fiona wondered why it was such a secret, but she respected Ransom's request and paused as the waitress showed him the bottle of wine and then opened it. She poured a glass for him to taste.

"Please pour a sample for Fi," Ransom said after he sipped.

Tammy did, and Fiona sipped and nodded. "That will be perfect with the meal."

Tammy filled their glasses and left again.

"My staff don't know about Liaisons, and I'd like to keep it that way. Jon may not have a problem with his employees being members, but I know my staff couldn't afford it and, frankly, I would rather not know about that side of their personal lives."

"Since you mentioned that, I presume it is expensive to join?"

"Yes. What other questions do you have?"

Fiona thought. He'd answered most of her questions. The biggest ones pertained to them being a couple. "Since we're getting back together, which we need to talk about too, would you go there by yourself?"

"Only if you were okay with it. But Fi, I wouldn't do anything there in the playrooms. Jon comes in without Angie and he doesn't go into a playroom without her. I assume Steven and Nicole would be the same, but the club has been largely closed since they got together because of the fire."

"I guess that leads to another question. If there have been so many problems, why did you guys decide to reopen? Why not just take the loss and move on?"

"It was a significant sum of money we invested. But also, we just couldn't do that to the other members. Liaisons has been open for over one hundred years."

Fiona choked on her water. "What?"

"Yes. When the fire happened, we found the original creator's papers."

"Why did they open it?"

He shook his head. Fiona guessed it was because someone was approaching the table. Sure enough, Tammy placed a salad plate in front of each of them.

"Truthfully," Ransom stated when the other woman left, "it was more to present them a place to cheat on their wives. There also might have been some members who weren't socially acceptable at that time. Remember, society didn't widely accept homosexuality until more recently. Think about that in the 1800s."

Fiona didn't have to. Knowing some of the issues still going on today, she easily imagined it was a lot more difficult back then.

"Okay, so how did it become what it is today?"

"That occurred a lot later. We suspect it was the financial burden during the Great Depression. When they offered memberships to help offset the costs, their money stretched a lot further."

Fiona ate her salad and processed some of what he said.

"Fi, look at me," Ransom said.

She raised her gaze and found him studying her.

"I'd like to take you there one night after the club resumes operations. I want you to see that it isn't what I know you think it is."

"I want you to do that. But I..."

"I know. No group stuff."

She felt her cheeks flush.

"Or maybe group stuff?" he questioned.

She felt the warmth spread.

"Interesting," he said before he took a sip of his wine. However, he wasn't sure he liked the idea of sharing her. That would be something he would have to seriously think about.

Fiona turned her attention back to salad and ate.

"Ransom?" A server approached the table. "We have an extremely upset customer demanding to see the owner."

Fiona tuned out whatever the problem was and thought about Ransom's question. Was she interested in something more than just a typical sexual experience? She never really thought about it. But that was because it had never been an option before.

"I'll be right back," Ransom said, interrupting her thoughts.

She nodded and sipped from her wine glass. While he was gone, she reviewed his answers to her questions so far. Ransom had always been transparent. He wasn't one to keep secrets even though he was keeping one now—and she had to admit to herself that she still felt guilty that she hadn't told him the truth about her parents yet. But what a person did in their private life was their business. The situation with her parents was different. She understood the separation of work and personal life. Particularly if it came to one's sexual activities. However, she honestly couldn't see how Liaisons would fit into their relationship. They had always had a rather experimental sex life in the past, but it never went beyond the two of them and some silk ties and blindfolds. Anything more than that had never interested them. At least for her. Had it always interested Ransom?

It sounded like Ransom wanted, or needed, more in that regard. The big question was, did she want more than what they had before? And that was something she just did not know. And truthfully, something that they didn't necessarily have to address until they committed completely to each other. They both admitted last night that they wanted to be together. But they still hadn't said that they actually would be. Yes, something like this figured into the discussion, but they could address that when it happened. If it happened. She knew she had hurt him before when she walked away, but she didn't know that she had hurt him as much as he said she did. After all, he'd been screwing the blonde within months. Sure, guys were a little different when it came to sex, but still. She figured he would have mourned the relationship longer if she had hurt him as badly as he said she had.

Ransom sank back in his chair, shaking his head as Tammy set their entrées on the table.

"Everything okay?"

"There are some people you can never satisfy. I just comped a three-hundred-dollar tab because the guy is a jerk."

"What? Why would you do that?"

"To get them to leave."

"But they'll just do it again."

"They won't here. I agreed to comp the meal on the condition that they never return."

"Ran," Fiona gasped. "What about reviews?"

"Fi, the reviews for the restaurant speak for themselves. There are many loyal customers who will challenge any negative review. Many of them are here tonight and witnessed the table causing the problem. Trust me, if the problem customer posts a bad review, those customers will quickly comment about what they witnessed, effectively negating the bad review. I can have it removed after a certain amount of time as well."

When Fiona was about to ask what happened, Ransom said, "Now, let's get back to our evening."

They sat in companionable silence and ate most of their meal.

Fiona asked, "The blonde I saw you with in your living room. Is she a member of Liaisons?"

Ransom was already shaking his head as she finished the question. "No, she wasn't. I've had no one from Liaisons at my home. Not even the other three owners."

"Where did you meet her?"

"At a bar. I hadn't reinstated my membership at Liaisons yet. I did the day after I slept with her."

"How long did you see her?"

"Just that one night," he said before he sipped his wine. "Where did you meet the guys you dated?"

"Friends arranged most of them. One was the coach of one athlete I worked with. But that didn't start until I finished the contract," she answered, realizing that it was unfair to hold him to a higher standard than she held herself. She certainly hadn't remained single any of the times they had split up, and he knew it from their argument last night. Hell, she had even agreed to marry one of them. However, it always took her several months to jump back into the dating pool after she left Ransom.

"Speaking of your athletes. What's going on with the situation here?" he asked before he wiped his mouth on his napkin and set it on the table.

"I terminated the contract with the original athlete. But the coach had someone else who could benefit from my services. The family is working on getting a deposit together. Once they get half, I'll start working with the athlete. It's a tough situation for the second athlete. It's a rough home life. The coach suggested some charities that might help with the fees and admitted if it came to it, he would pay it. He always felt the second athlete could use my services more than the first athlete, anyway. I observed the athlete earlier last week and there's a lot of potential."

"So, you'll remain in Charleston? What about your parents?" he asked as he pulled his phone from his pocket. "Sorry," he said, glancing at the screen. "Oh no," he said.

"What?" she asked, setting her fork on her now empty plate, secretly relieved for the interruption so she could skirt the question about her parents. That will come in time; this wasn't the time.

As she wiped her mouth, she thought about the meal. It was fantastic. Ransom had found a talented chef for the restaurant.

"It's from Steven. He and Nicole are at the hospital."

"What?"

"It looks like she's miscarrying," he said as his fingers flew over the screen as he typed out a message.

"Did you know she was pregnant? Do you need to go?" she asked. She stopped herself from asking if they should go.

"I just asked him. Let's see what he says. And no, I didn't know she was pregnant."

Tammy showed up at the table then. "Any dessert for you two tonight?"

"No," Ransom and Fiona said at the same time.

"Will you put the wine away for me? We'll get it later," Ransom said, reading a message on his phone.

"Sure," Tammy said. Taking the bottle and reinserting the cork. "The usual spot?"

"Yes," Ransom said, standing. "Thanks Tammy."

Ransom walked to Fiona's chair before she could stand, and he pulled it out. Fiona rose and grabbed her purse from where it rested on the edge of the table.

"Something has come up. We need to leave," he said in explanation. "I'll come back with your tip later, okay?"

Tammy nodded.

Fiona followed him out the back of the restaurant and climbed into the passenger seat after Ransom opened the door.

"Are you going to the hospital?" she asked once he had backed out of the parking spot.

"We're going," he said, "he asked for us to come."

"I didn't realize you two were that close," Fiona said.

"We're not close enough to hang out and watch football together, but we are friends. At least I like to think we are. We'll go check on them and we can swing back by and grab what's left in the bottle and head to your place to finish it."

Fiona knew he suggested her place because Ransom never drank at his house. He wouldn't want the wine there at all. It was a boundary she respected.

"We could take the bottle with us now and you can drive me home before you go check on them," she offered.

"It's just easier if you come with me."

Fiona stopped arguing. Besides, she was a little curious about his relationship with the other owners. She had seen very little between them besides business earlier today. If they had done what she knew they had, she figured they would have more than just a business relationship.

"How often do you think people from Liaisons interact outside of the club together?"

"I don't know. I've always had pretty firm boundaries. What happened there, stayed there. The other owners and I have had some business-related meetings outside of those walls, but it was because of what was happening at that time."

His phone made a noise. He handed it to Nicole. "Tell me what it says."

"What's the code?"

"Your birthday," he said.

"What?" she said, entering the numbers.

"No one could ever guess that one," he said with a shrug of his shoulders.

She opened the messaging app. "He said thank you."

"Send back anytime," Ransom said as he watched for a break in traffic to turn left.

Fiona replied and held onto the phone in case anything else came in. When they arrived at the hospital ten minutes later, they found Steven and Jon sitting in the waiting room of the emergency department.

"Angie still has connections here, even if she isn't working here anymore. She's gone back to check on Nicole," Jon said.

"Why aren't you back there, Steven?" Ransom asked.

"They were examining her and talking about surgery, but I didn't understand why. They asked me to leave, so I came out here to wait."

Based on his tone, Fiona knew the hospital staff had essentially forced him to leave the room. Being out here was torturing him.

"She wants kids so bad," Steven whispered as he put his head in his hands and rested his elbows on his knees.

She didn't hear what Jon or Ransom said because she caught sight of Angie coming down the hall. Fiona walked to meet her to give the guys some privacy.

"Hey," Fiona said.

"Hey. Glad you guys are here. The doctor's coming out in a minute. It isn't good news."

"What did they say?" Steven commanded, clearly having heard what Angie said.

"He's coming out to talk to you," Angie said. "Hang on."

"Tell me, Angie," Steven insisted.

"She has an ectopic pregnancy."

"What does that mean?" Steven demanded again.

"The embryo is in her fallopian tube. They have to go in and remove it."

"She won't have the baby?"

Angie gave her head a slow shake. Fiona's heart tightened at the sadness on Steven's face. In her opinion, after seeing that reaction, Nicole wasn't the only one who wanted kids.

A doctor emerged from the hall where Angie had come from.

"Mr. Cavanaugh?"

Steven stood.

"Ms. St. James said I could update you. We need to take her to surgery. She has an ectopic pregnancy, which has led to severe stress on her fallopian tube. From the ultrasound, it's possible it has already ruptured the tube, but it's not clear. We're going to see if we can repair it, but I can't promise that. I've already told her that. She's asking for you, but the sooner we take her up, the better, especially if it hasn't ruptured the tube. If you come with me, I'll give you a few minutes with her while they prep the OR. But it won't be a long visit."

"We'll wait until you get back," Angie said. "Then you can tell us if you want us to stay with you."

The four sat in silence waiting for Steven to return.

———

Thew news that Nicole was pregnant shocked Ransom. They had learned it the day of Angie and Jon's engagement party. Steven had explained they hadn't wanted to take away from Jon and Angie's moment.

He wondered how Fiona felt. He reached for her hand and held it tight. No one had been by her side when the doctors provided her with Hope's diagnosis. Was this bringing back memories for her?

Steven returned a few brief minutes later.

"They took her up. I need to call her parents," he said, running his hand through his hair.

"Call them. We'll wait," Angie said.

"No, you guys go home. It'll be easier to tell them without distractions."

"Steven—" Angie began.

"I know you mean well, Angie, but it's better for me to be alone right now. Barring complications, the doctor said the surgery shouldn't take more than a couple of hours."

"You'll let us know if you want us to come back," Ransom said. While they hadn't really been much support for each other outside of Liaisons-associated business, he wanted to think of them as friends, not just business partners. Hell, they had seen each other naked countless times. If that didn't constitute some kind of friendship, what did?

"I will," Steven said. "I'll also let you know when she's out of surgery. I appreciate you guys coming. I..." he trailed off. "I know we've never had much of a relationship outside of Liaisons but thank you for coming."

Mac walked in at that moment. "What's going on?"

A quick summary of what had happened took place with Angie adding a few points Steven missed.

"I'm staying with you," Mac said. "No arguments. You can make your calls, but you don't need to wait alone."

"We tried to tell him that," Angie and Jon said in unison.

A melancholic smile curved Steven's lip. "Mac can wait with me. The rest of you carry on with your evening. Thank you again for coming."

"Text or call when you know something," Ransom said. "I'll be back here in a flash."

Steven simply nodded.

Ransom, Fiona, Jon and Angie left at the same time. They stopped once they were outside the hospital.

"We were at the restaurant when I got the text. I think we're going to go back there and finish the bottle of wine we opened. You two are welcome to join us," Ransom said.

"Sure," Jon said after he exchanged a look with Angie. "I think that might be good while we wait to see if we need to return. Besides, Angie and I haven't eaten dinner yet."

"I'll call and get them to set us up a table," Ransom said, extracting his phone from his pocket. "Do you know what you want, since the kitchen closes soon?"

"Whatever they have that is quick to prepare is fine with me," Angie said.

Jon nodded his agreement.

Ransom quickly thought about what the two usually ate when at the restaurant. "We had a tuna steak special tonight. If they have any left, does that sound like something you'd eat?"

"Fine with me," Jon said. "If not, I'll take the fried chicken."

"I agree, but I'd rather have the seafood salad if they don't have the special left," Angie said.

"Done. See you there," Ransom said, raising his phone to his ear as he led Fiona to the car.

He was concerned that she had spoken very little while they had been at the hospital.

He completed his phone call while they walked to the car. The hostess said the front booth was available and would get the kitchen working on the chicken and the salad since they had sold out of the special ten minutes earlier.

As he exited the parking lot he said, "Fi, are you okay?"

"Yeah. I just feel for them. I get the sense Nicole really wants children, and I wonder what this will do to her ability to have them. I was also thinking how I wish, looking back, that I hadn't handled the situation with Hope mostly on my own. Sure, Greg was there too, but I know I shut him out for a while. I remember wishing that you were there. I'm sorry," she said.

Ransom heard her choke on the last word. He reached over and clasped her hand and raised it to his lips. "I wish I'd been there too."

"I'm sorry I denied you that," she said.

Ransom glanced at her and with the help of the headlights of a passing car, he saw the tears coming from her eyes.

"Fi, I don't want to say it's okay, because part of me says it's not. But you did what you thought was best. Am I happy with it? No. Do I understand it? Yes, to a certain degree. I just wish I could have been there to hold you. I wish I could have held her once before she was gone. I don't say that to make you feel guilty. I say it because it's true."

She squeezed his hand; he squeezed hers back.

"Dry your eyes, honey. Yes, we still need to talk about it, but not tonight. Or at least not right now or at the restaurant."

He spoke the truth. They still needed to deal with that without all the emotion of last night, but this wasn't the time or the place to do it.

When they walked back into the almost empty restaurant, they found Jon and Angie seated at the front booth where they could see the street. Four glasses of water sat on the table along with the bottle of wine from earlier in a chiller. Just after Ransom and Fiona sat, Tammy brought two drinks and two empty wine glasses over. She set what Ransom suspected was Vodka in front of Angie and what he knew was Scotch in front of Jon. Then filled the two empty wine glasses for he and Fiona.

"I'll bring the food in just a moment. They were plating it last time I was in the kitchen," Tammy said and disappeared.

The four sipped in silence.

"Who knew?" Angie finally asked.

"We didn't," Ransom said.

"This whole thing tonight drove something home for me," Jon said. "Even though we've known each other for years, we never *really* knew what was going on in each other's lives until more recently."

"I agree," Ransom said. "Business wise, the four of us know a lot about each other. Personally, we know very little."

"Like you winning several Olympic medals?" Jon said.

Ransom smiled.

"What?" Angie asked.

"It's how I met Fiona. We were on four Olympic teams together. Fiona was a gymnast. I was a swimmer."

"Wow," Angie said. "Now I know why you looked familiar, Fiona. You're from Charleston, right? I've lived here all my life."

Fiona smiled. "Yes, I lived here for a while. Being on the team was a once in a lifetime experience. One I'd never trade for anything."

That ignited a conversation that lasted through the rest of the bottle of wine plus an additional glass for each of them while Jon and Angie ate their meal and joined them for a second drink in the now empty restaurant. Ransom sent the staff home and locked the door an hour earlier. Jon and Ransom, along with Fiona and Angie, had established a genuine friendship by the time they left.

Back in the car, Ransom drove them to Fiona's apartment and followed her up the stairs.

Once inside, before she could say anything, he pulled her into his arms and kissed her.

He felt her surprise when she stiffened, and when he was about to let her go, she relaxed, wrapped her arms around him, and opened her mouth.

He pulled her closer, so every inch of them touched. He wanted her. He'd wanted her all day. He backed her down the short hallway to her bedroom and then followed her down to the bed. This would be more than what they had last night.

Slowly, he caressed and stripped her of her clothing as she helped to shed his from him. The only sounds in the apartment were their soft pants and moans.

When he finally slid within her, he knew he could never let her go again.

"Be with me, Fi. Be mine," he whispered against her lips as he drove rhythmically into her. "You've always been mine. Be mine again."

"Yes," she breathed against his lips and then fell over the edge.

He wanted more. He slowed his movements to allow her to enjoy the moment. Then picked up the pace and brought her to completion again, just as he experienced his own.

18

────

A week later...

Jon Vargas: We need to meet. All four of us. ASAP.

Ransom groaned when he saw the text message. The club had barely been open for a week. What could possibly have gone wrong already?

Ransom: An hour?

That would give him time to swim and shower before meeting them.

Jon's response was immediate.

Jon Vargas: Fine. We're already at the club.

The 'fine' conveyed Jon wasn't happy about something.

Ransom: Then I'm on my way. Be there in 20.

There were some short cuts Ransom knew he could take to get there quickly.

Jon Vargas: Room 4

Why room four?

After pulling on a T-shirt and shoving his feet into a pair of flip-flops, he grabbed his keys, wallet, and then headed out the door, still dressed in the swim trunks he had just put on before the phone pinged with the incoming text message. He had been about to do his laps for the day in hopes he could see Fiona tonight when she finished with her athlete.

However, an accident at one intersection forced him to detour, making his promised twenty minutes turn into thirty. Pulling into his parking spot behind the building, he wasted no time entering the club. He wanted to get this over with. Maybe he should let the others buy him out. Owning Liaisons was nowhere near as much fun as he thought it would be. Not that he thought it would be a walk in the park. He owned a restaurant; he knew nothing ran perfectly. But Liaisons should essentially take care of itself, and it took up a lot of his time because it wasn't running itself.

He went straight to room four and saw a sign attached to the door that said the room was unavailable until further notice.

"What the hell?" he asked, reaching for the doorknob.

He heard the low voices of the other three as soon as he entered. However, what they were saying wasn't what caught his attention. What grabbed his attention was the fact that the room was in shambles. Furniture overturned, some pieces broken, and the mattress slashed open. The harness still hung from the pole but was no longer functional. Studying the fabric strewn around the room, he realized it was the linens for the room, all shredded and beyond use.

"What happened?" he demanded.

"That's what we'd like to know?" Mac said.

"Well, isn't that what the cameras are for?" Ransom asked in a sarcastic tone.

"Funny you should say that," Jon said, raising the tablet he held in his hand.

Ransom had a bad feeling settle in his stomach.

"Did you tell Fiona about us in this room?" Steven asked.

Ransom didn't hesitate. "Yes, but—"

"Did you tell her about us being with Angie in this room?" Steven asked, a harsh edge to his tone.

"No," he said. Because he had chosen not to tell her yet. "I debated about telling her," he admitted. "But I didn't think Nicole knew the four of us had been with Angie that time, and I didn't want Fi to slip and say something."

Steven muttered something under his breath that Ransom couldn't hear.

"What was that?" Ransom insisted, his temper igniting.

"Nicole fucking knows," Steven practically shouted. "We had one hell of a fight this morning."

"Not because of me, I assure you," Ransom said. "Why do you ask about Fiona knowing?"

Jon held up the tablet again. "How do you think?"

The cameras. Of course. "Fi didn't do this," Ransom said, gesturing at the destruction around them. "Could it have been Nicole?" Ransom asked. It made sense, especially if she was angry at Steven for not telling her about being with Angie.

Steven snarled and stepped towards Ransom. Jon and Mac positioned themselves between them, halting Steven's progress. Mac faced Steven, and Jon faced Ransom.

"The cameras say otherwise," Mac murmured over his shoulder, his hand braced against Steven's chest.

"Fiona couldn't have. She hasn't been here since the day we inspected the inventory. She didn't want to come. Besides, someone would have had to sign her in at the front."

"He has a point there," Mac said, again over his shoulder. "If she came in the front."

Ransom hated that comment because it implied that someone had some in via the back.

"She came in the back," Jon said.

"How? She'd have to..." Ransom said, and then his memory kicked in. He hadn't hidden his door code from her the day she came with him.

"Exactly. She saw your code," Steven said.

"This doesn't make sense. Why would she come in here and do this?"

"Jealousy?" Jon said.

"Of what? We're barely back together."

"You're sharing a bed, aren't you?" Mac said, his eyes still on Steven.

"But that doesn't mean she'd do this," Ransom argued. "Show me the video."

The four faced each other.

Jon handed the tablet to Ransom.

"Push the play button. It's all the footage from when she came in the back door."

"And you verified it was my code that was used?" Ransom asked, taking the tablet.

"It was," Jon said. "I already had Maverick double check it."

Ransom hit play and watched as a slight figure—the same height and build as Fiona—wearing a black hoodie slipped in the back door and walked down the hall. The hood was up, but he could clearly see a lock of red hair peeking out of one side. He watched the person go straight to the room they were in and open the door. The next shot was of her in the room. She examined the room for a split second before she started rummaging through the bureaus and chests, emptying the contents out as she went. After emptying those, she pushed at the furniture until each one toppled over. He watched as the destruction continued. Then she pulled something from the pocket of the hoodie and flipped it open. A knife—and a serious looking one at that. That was when she went after the mattress, linens, and finally, the harness.

"I can't believe it," he mumbled as he handed the tablet back to Jon.

"Cameras don't lie," Jon said.

"No, they don't," Ransom agreed. But something was bothering him. Something about the video didn't fit with Fiona.

He trusted these men. He knew they wouldn't set Fiona up. But someone did. Someone who had red hair and a—

"Give me that back," he said, reaching for the tablet.

"Why?" Jon said, holding the tablet out of reach.

"Just play it back. Better yet, can we use a bigger screen, or can you zoom in on that thing?"

"Let's go to the office," Jon said. "We can bring it up on the television there."

They filed out of the room, and Jon locked the door behind them. Ransom felt the tension radiating from Steven. He knew Steven was anxious about Nicole, but why was he so angry at Ransom?

Ransom knew it couldn't be Fiona in the video.

Their new office was where Nicole had found the papers they had been looking for before the fire. It was better suited for an office. They combined some of the smaller playrooms during the renovation and converted their old office space back into a playroom.

Jon set up the laptop and established a connection with the television so they could view the entire video again.

When they reached the part where the woman extracted the knife from her pocket was when Ransom said to pause it.

"There, on the right wrist. It's a tattoo. Fiona doesn't have any tattoos," he said, pointing at the screen.

"That could be a string from the hoodie," Steven argued.

"Jon, can you zoom in?" Ransom asked.

"Already on it," Jon said, hitting a few keys on the keyboard of the laptop that sat on the conference table.

He adjusted the screen to enlarge and centered it on the wrist.

"That's not a string," Mac said, examining the image.

"I agree," Jon said.

"There's too much detail to be just a string," Ransom said. "It's not Fiona. Is there another angle to get a shot of the person's face?"

"No. I already checked. The hoodie covers too much to give any facial detail. I doubt any enhancing program will help," Jon said.

"Can you zoom in on the left ankle?" Mac said.

Jon mashed some more buttons, and, in an instant, the left ankle was centered on the screen.

"Another tattoo," Jon said.

Ransom studied the tattoo on the screen. From the angle, it reminded him of the tribal bands that most people got around their biceps.

Jon redirected his focus to Ransom and Mac. "Is there someone you two declined to go into that room with?"

Ransom and Mac both shook their heads.

"The last time I was in that room," Mac said, "was with Lyra, Maverick, and Ransom. Before the fire."

"That's the last time I was in that room as well," Ransom said. "Well, outside of checking the inventory with Fiona."

"That's not Lyra?" Steven asked.

"No, she doesn't have any tattoos," Ransom said.

"Besides, she's a blonde," Mac added.

"What about Tank and Maverick? Anyone know if they've turned down a woman?" Steven asked.

"I wouldn't know. I haven't talked to them," Mac said.

Ransom was confused. "When did Tank become a member?" he asked.

Jon said, "After we reopened. I don't think he's been in that room yet."

"How do you feel about that?" Ransom asked. He had always wanted to know how Jon felt about his employees being members. Jon was Tank and Maverick's boss.

"I don't spend all that much time here anymore, at least not without Angie. Besides, what my employees do with their down time is their business, provided it isn't illegal. That's why I had no issue with Maverick joining after Angie's shooting. Any of my employees are welcome to join if they can afford it."

"Something else to consider," Mac said. "Is there an individual we recently denied membership but could attend a few times as a guest? This is certainly something someone like that might do."

"Possible. But that might be someone going back years," Jon said. "How many women did the four of us, or five if you count Maverick when I stopped, have in that room?"

"How did they know my code?" Ransom asked.

"And how many other members have been in that room in a similar capacity?" Mac asked, apparently ignoring Ransom's question.

Ransom's code was also Fiona's birthday, which no one could connect to him as far as he knew.

"Could it be someone we denied employment?" Ransom asked.

"Is this related to the other problems we've had?" Steven asked at the same time.

"It's possible, would be the correct answer to all of those questions," Jon said.

"Hence my question. This feels very targeted to us, or at least the people that use this room for group interactions," Mac said. "It could have been someone upset about being excluded from some playtime."

The four of them tried not to use the word orgy because that wasn't the only thing that happened in that room—like the four of them pleasuring one woman. One really wouldn't call that an orgy technically, at least in Ransom's mind. In his mind, an orgy was when a bunch of people were just having sex in the same room, and possibly interacting with each other. Meaning they pleasured each other. That isn't what happened when he was in this room with these men. They didn't interact with each other outside of who was where.

"It could be someone whose partner just found out they're a member here and maybe that person joined in activities in that room," Ransom said.

"So, we're back to the question of who the target was here. Us, including Maverick, or the club?" Jon said.

"Or we have a breach of confidentiality," Steven said.

"It could be someone who's going through a separation and their partner found out about them being a member," Ransom said. "Going back to Mac's idea about someone's partner doing this."

"True," Steven said.

"Another question. Do we want to involve the police?" Mac said. "It didn't look like she wore gloves. There could be fingerprints on the things she touched."

"What if I had someone from RLS come in and fingerprint the room? There couldn't be that many since we reopened," Jon said.

"Not Tank or Maverick," Steven said.

"No, I'd get someone who isn't a member," Jon said. "Besides, Tank and Maverick's fingerprints could be in the room. I only looked at the footage that was dumped from that room around the time the cleaning crew notified the managers on duty. The managers called me since I can access the cameras from RLS. I really think I would need more of a reason than this to look at the footage of the other people using that room."

Ransom agreed. None of them wanted to invade the privacy of the other members just to see if they could spot a woman with red hair with tattoos on her wrist and ankle.

"If we have RLS do it, and we find out who it is, could we press charges without the police being involved now?" Ransom asked. "And could someone you trust review the camera from the common areas and look for the woman?"

"I think we could get around that a little. If Liaisons hires RLS to do an investigation, and the investigation is above board, I think we could hand the information over to the police without issue," Mac said.

Ever the attorney, Ransom thought. But he agreed with Mac's idea.

"Then why don't we do that? I think keeping the police out as long as we can is a good thing. They're already very interested in what goes on here," Steven said. And he would know, as the police had implicated him in Mandy's murder—whom the four of them had spent time with many times, both individually and as a group. Steven also had been the top suspect in setting the fire that caused extensive damage to most of the playrooms. The investigators had yet to exonerate him of the murder, but they also had failed to charge him. The four of them were confident that the police would soon clear the arson charge completely as well. Ransom knew Steven hadn't committed either crime. It just wasn't in his nature. Besides, Steven wrote true crime books. If he wanted to do it, he could certainly guarantee that nothing linked back to him.

"I still think it strange that most of this started when we started making offers to buy Liaisons," Mac said. "The situation with Jon and Angie may have ended here at the club, but there were already incidents occurring with things like security and someone accessing the cameras, especially in relation to Jon and Angie."

"You think it's someone worried about the four of us owning Liaisons?" Steven asked.

"I think it looks like that," Mac said.

"Someone we've been with?" Jon said.

"Possibly," Ransom and Steven said at the same time.

"Likely," Mac said.

"Who told Nicole?" Ransom asked.

"It was in a card that arrived with a bouquet of flowers," Steven said.

"She thought they were from you," Ransom said. He didn't need to ask. Who else would send Steven's girlfriend flowers? Especially after the lost pregnancy and her surgery last week.

"Yes."

"How did they know about us and Angie? There are only five people who know that happened and four of us are here. The fifth has been recovering from a gunshot wound that nearly killed her," Mac said.

"Would you let us read the card?" Jon asked.

Ransom studied Steven as the other man thought.

"I'll ask her. She's," he paused, visibly debating about sharing something else, "not herself since the hospital and the surgery. The ectopic pregnancy hit her hard. She wants children so bad..." After a pause, Steven said, "I'm sorry about earlier. You were protecting your girl. It's been stressful since the surgery."

"And I know you were standing up for yours. I'm sorry, too. I know Nicole couldn't have done something like this," Ransom said. Even though he barely knew Nicole, he sincerely believed what had happened wasn't something Nicole would do. Not when she had her own issues that were also connected to the club. Certainly not when someone had embezzled millions of dollars from the accounting firm Nicole formerly worked for and had made it look like she had done it. Most of the money that person had taken came from Liaisons. She was also instrumental in getting the money back. In fact, she was still their accountant; she was opening her own firm and the four of them had readily agreed that she should remain their accountant.

Even if she was upset about Steven having been sexually involved with someone she knew—even if it was a rather recent introduction—she wouldn't have gone after Liaisons. She would have vented her anger on Steven. And from Steven's earlier reaction, it seemed like she certainly had.

"Alright, now that we've all kissed and made up," Jon interrupted, "we're good with RLS doing the investigation? I could have Allison do it. I know she's not a member and would lend a female's point of view to the situation. Since the person on the video appears to be female."

"Yes," the other three said in unison.

"I'll call her. For now, that room remains unavailable and locked. Regarding the other members, we can issue a memo that something failed in the room following the renovation and it's closed for safety purposes. It might lead them to question the safety of other rooms, but we'll deal with it if it happens."

No one argued.

———

Upon leaving Liaisons, and the issues in the hands of the others, Ransom decided he needed a day out on the water, and it had been far too long since he had last enjoyed one. The meeting with Jon, Mac, and Steven had been intense. The damage was troubling. How did a club that was staffed twenty-four-seven have this many issues?

What better way to escape than an afternoon on the water with Fiona? He pulled out his phone to text her while stopped at a red light.

Ransom: Taking the boat out for a few hours. Join me?

He set his phone down and waited for the light to turn green as his thoughts returned to the issues at Liaisons. There was no clear connection between all the problems lately, but there had to be one. There was no other explanation.

He heard his phone ding, but since he was driving, he left it resting in the cup holder until he got someplace where he could safely read it. It was one reason he wished he didn't own a collectible car. While he loved the late 1990s Aston Martin Vantage DB7, he really would like the ability to have his car read his texts to him and then be able to respond. He'd also really love to have Bluetooth in it. The car was the one thing he still had of his father's that the man had loved more than alcohol or drugs. Ransom just refused to have anything else right now.

At the next intersection, the light turned yellow, so he stopped. Grabbing his phone, he saw a text from Fiona.

Fiona Campbell: Sure. Let me know where to meet you. I can be there in half an hour.

He activated the dictation feature and responded with what marina and the slip to meet him at. He hit send just when the light turned green. Returning the phone back down to the cup holder, he took his foot off the brake and drove through the intersection and continued to the marina.

At the marina, he hit the small store and grabbed a case of bottled water, ice for the cooler he kept on the boat, and some sandwiches since he had yet to eat today.

He made his way down to his slip where the wake boat he splurged on several years back with some of the endorsement money he had earned when he was an Olympic athlete. He had even been a spokesperson for the boat company for a while. It was the only thing he had ever splurged on besides his bungalow.

Once on the boat, he filled the onboard cooler with some of the water bottles before adding the ice, then he added a few more bottles and the sandwiches. He stowed the leftover bottles for future use. He would likely just take them home and use them when he went to the gym rather than leave them on the boat. Despite being sealed up, water that experienced temperature fluctuations from hot to cold and then hot again wasn't a good thing.

As he was examining the boat before heading out, he thought about what he wanted from Fiona. It had only been a week since she agreed they would be together. And what a spectacular moment it had been. He had buried himself deep in her and, even though he said he would never do it, he had begged her to be his again. She agreed. They had even talked after about being together and making plans for her to consider moving back to Charleston permanently. They had seen each other every day and truthfully had ended up in bed more often than not. But being in bed was never their issue. It was always out of it that complicated things. But they would work through those issues.

While leaning over the back of the boat to inspect the engine, he noticed something that seemed out of place. There was another wire that he didn't remember being there before. Before he could examine it more closely, he heard his name called.

Looking up, he saw Fiona walking down the long marina boardwalk. He waved.

Next thing he knew, he was flying through the air. The last thing that crossed his mind was that he would never hold Fiona again.

19

Fiona stared in horror as the boat burst into flames. Pieces of fiberglass and who knew what else flew into the air and then splashed into the water. She dropped to the worn boards of the boardwalk and shielded her head as she screamed, "Ransom!"

The boardwalk shook as more boats exploded. Fiona couldn't hear herself think over the noise. Then another two booms assaulted her ears.

What was happening?

Curled in a ball, with her hands still over her head, she kept screaming for Ransom. Everything she dreaded just happened. The one thing she wanted in this entire world, besides having her baby girl back, was gone.

Tears flowed from her eyes. Someone grabbed her leg, and she kicked out then curled back up into a ball.

"Lady, we gotta get out of here!"

Fiona heard the words but there was nothing on this earth that would make herself respond whoever it was.

She started crying. He was gone. Ransom was gone.

"She won't move!" the person yelled.

Two muscular arms wrapped around her, hauled her to her feet before tossing her over a broad shoulder in a fireman's carry before carting her away from the inferno that surrounded her.

Helplessly, she extended her arms out and gazed towards where Ransom's boat had been. There was nothing but flames.

The person carried her back to the marina parking area as the flashing lights of the first responders' vehicles arrived. She vaguely noticed someone busy near the gas pumps working to keep them from exploding, too. A part of her mind wondered why they had arrived so quickly, even though she had no concept of time. It still seemed like they'd arrived way too fast.

Fiona didn't register the passage of time, but her tears slowed at some point. When someone pressed a gauze pad to her forehead, she hissed in pain.

"It's okay. You're fine, but we need to get this cut cleaned. There's no telling what's in it," the person said.

She shifted her gaze from the burning boats and fixated on the woman in front of her. The uniform designated her as EMS.

"Are you hurt anywhere else?"

"No. At least I don't think so," Fiona managed to say. "Has anyone found Ransom?"

"What?"

"Montgomery Ransom. He was on his boat. I was meeting him. His boat," she sobbed, tears falling anew, "was the first to explode. Has anyone found his body?"

"There was someone on a boat? We were told there was no one down there but you."

"He was on the boat," she sobbed, then hiccupped. "He couldn't have survived that, could he?"

"Ma'am, there are at least ten boats burning down there. We know there were at least two explosions, but debris landed on several others and caught them on fire."

"There were three different booms," Fiona said. She knew that much, at least. "The first was Ransom's boat. I couldn't tell you how many with the other two booms."

"That's good. Is there anything else you remember?" the EMS worker asked. "Anything at all could help them. Did you see anyone else?"

"No, just," she paused on another hiccup/sob. Then begged, "Please? I need to know about Ransom."

"I'll get someone over. Can you give a description of this person?"

"Yes," she sniffed and brushed away her tears.

"Okay. I'll get someone. Can we call anyone? I really think you should go to the hospital."

Fiona shook her head before the EMS worker finished the last sentence. "No hospital. I'm staying here. I can't call his family until we know more. Just let me stay here."

And she did. She watched the firefighters battle the burning boats and marina. Someone came over to get a description of Ransom. She vaguely remembered taking out her phone and looking for a picture of him. She knew it wasn't a recent one, but it was damn close enough in her opinion.

At some point, she pulled her phone back out to check the time. Four hours had gone by since she arrived at the marina. And she had a text message from an unknown number over an hour ago.

Unknown number: This is Jon. I saw the news about the marina. I think Ransom houses a boat there. Do you know where Ransom is? He isn't answering his phone.

Instead of answering the text, she hit the information button and called him.

"Fiona?"

"Jon," she cried as her tears continued to flow.

"What's happened?"

Quickly, and as best as she could between sobs and hiccups, she explained what had happened.

"I'm on my way. Are you okay?"

"I need to know about Ransom. I can't take another one gone," she wept.

"Can I call someone?"

"I don't want to call his mom or sisters until I know more," she exclaimed, half registering that she was bordering on hysteria.

"I understand. I'll be there as soon as I can. Can I bring you anything?"

"No," she sobbed. "I'm relatively okay."

"What does that mean?"

"Emotionally, I'm shit, Jon. How's that?" she snapped. "But physically, I'm fine."

She thought she heard him chuckle.

"I'm leaving now. I'll find you when I get there." Then the call disconnected.

Fiona was numb. She couldn't feel anything. She thought, at this moment, she would feel grief, or sadness, or even fear. Instead, she couldn't feel her fingers, toes, the tip of her nose, or the spot on her head where she had hit the deck on the boardwalk.

So, this is what shock felt like.

She stared at the firefighters, who were still working to douse the flames.

She jumped when a hand touched her right shoulder.

Jon smiled a sad smile when she glanced at him.

"Hey. Are you okay?"

"I don't know," she admitted in a whisper.

"Fiona?"

She turned to look to her left and saw Angie standing there. Fiona didn't know why, but she flung herself at Angie and started crying anew. Angie wrapped her in a firm hug. Fiona heard a slight hiss of pain. She didn't register whether it was her or Angie but tightened her grip around Angie. Angie said nothing. Just held tight.

"Come on. Let's get you out of here. There's nothing more you can do tonight," Angie murmured countless minutes later. Fiona was unaware of how long she'd cried as the other woman held her.

Fiona shook her head against Angie's chest. "No, I'm not going anywhere until—"

"They have a description of him. They're searching the water," Angie said. "Let's go. Jon has already requested an update. He's good at stuff like that. He has contacts all over this city within law enforcement and EMS."

"I have to be here when they find him," Fiona argued.

"Fiona, you need food and warmth. You're freezing. You're in shock. Sitting here in this state won't help Ransom one bit."

Fiona, aware deep down that Angie was right, straightened and allowed Jon and Angie to lead her from the scene she would always remember as the end of her life as she knew it.

20

Fiona huddled and shivered in an office chair in a warehouse that Angie said was Jon's office building. Someone wrapped her in a blanket and handed her a cup of coffee. Taking a sip, she realized it was very strong and whoever had fixed it had added a heavy dose of Bailey's Irish Cream.

All around her, people were busy. She didn't know what they were doing, but she hoped they were aiding the search for Ransom's body. Of that, she knew. They were searching for a body. There was no way he survived that explosion.

"How's the coffee?"

Fiona turned to see Angie easing herself into the other chair next to her.

"Strong. You made it?" Fiona croaked.

"Yes. And even though you probably shouldn't have the alcohol, the Bailey's should help a little. Shock is a funny thing. Are you hurt anywhere else? I can check."

"They treated a scratch on my forehead. Besides some stinging on my knees, I'm fine," Fiona said, finally registering the pain in her knees.

"Let me check those. Marina boards are full of bacteria," Angie said.

That was when Fiona spotted the first aid kit on the table. Moving the blanket aside, she pulled up the hem of her long sundress to reveal her knees. Sure enough, there were some deep abrasions on both knees and on one of her thighs that corresponded with some tears in her dress.

"I thought so. Let me clean them for you," Angie said, opening the kit. "Last thing you need is some nasty infection."

Fiona nodded her agreement but wouldn't mind some nasty infection putting an end to her suffering at this point. She had no other reason in the world to live.

Angie opened the kit and started pulling out supplies.

"Tell me more about you two at the Olympics," Angie said as she donned a pair of surgical gloves before she ripped open an alcohol packet. "I don't think we mentioned the other night that the guys only recently learned that he'd been an Olympic athlete."

As Angie cleaned and bandaged the wounds, Fiona concentrated on talking about Ransom and sharing more memories of their times at the Olympics.

"You two dated?" Angie said, depositing all the used supplies in a biohazard bag, then took off the gloves she'd worn as she cleaned the wounds, adding them to the same bag and then knotting it tight. "The other night, we guessed, but we didn't want to ask outright."

"Several times," Fiona said, finishing the cup of coffee. "Three times before this one, in fact."

"So, you two are dating now?"

"Yes," Fiona said. "But we haven't told anyone yet because of our history."

"Relationships can be hard," Angie said.

"Ours was hard because of me. The first time it ended, we were both so young and the thought of being tied down, having experienced no one but him, terrified me," Fiona said. It was the first time she ever admitted it to anyone other than herself. "The other times, it's more complicated."

Angie laughed, but somehow Fiona knew Angie wasn't laughing at her. "Complications occur in all relationships," Angie said.

"True," Fiona agreed.

"Are you hungry? Jon has a canteen around the corner. It always has food stocked. I saw some sandwiches when I was fixing your coffee."

"I should eat something. I'm not even sure what time it is now," Fiona confessed, although she wasn't hungry.

"By that you mean you aren't hungry, but shock will do that to you. It would be good to eat something while we wait for news," Angie said. "I'll fix us some food and come back." Then Angie rose and took the medical supplies with her and disappeared.

Fiona returned to watching the flurry of activity around her. People were on the phones, running search programs, and occasionally walking over to Jon and another man she didn't know to give a report. At least, that was what she thought they were doing. She couldn't figure out what else the people in the room could focus on. But again, she was unsure about what Jon's company really did besides the cameras at Liaisons.

Liaisons. That brought back a whole different situation. They still hadn't talked about how it could or would fit into their relationship. She hadn't wanted to visit the club when it was open. Now she wished she had, just once, with him.

She wasn't sure how she felt about the place. She couldn't bear the idea of Ransom going there and participating in sexual activities with other people. And she sure as hell knew Ransom would never tolerate her engaging in sex with other people there either. After all, he had successfully blocked any potential date she could have had the last several months she had been in Charleston. Would they have gone there together? She didn't know that answer either. While she knew he had engaged in what some might call kinky acts, she knew that some things that happened there she definitely wasn't interested in. But she couldn't deny that she had fantasized about Ransom and certain things they could do to each other. He even took part in one where she had blindfolded him. They had played with some bondage with her, but her biggest fantasy was to have him bound but they had never done it. She couldn't quite see Ransom willingly surrendering all control to someone else. So instead, she did it verbally that one time by ordering him to hold on to the headboard. Could there have been more of that? Maybe. Would they have needed someplace besides their own bedroom to do it? Not necessarily.

But of course, all of that was moot now. Ran was dead.

Tears filled her eyes at that thought. Ran was dead. She was right. She had lost everyone she ever remotely cared about, outside of her parents, in accidents. But her parents were gone too, in a way. They had no clue who she was.

She would never love again. She would never have children. The unbearable pain shattered her soul. She would never go through this again. She would be alone for the rest of her life.

Holding her stomach, she leaned forward on a moan and started to cry.

"Oh no, Fiona, don't give up hope yet," Angie said and laid a hand against Fiona's back.

"You don't understand," Fiona sobbed.

"What don't I understand?" Angie asked.

Fiona looked at Angie.

"I have lost everyone I've ever cared about. That's why I ended the relationship before with Ran. I couldn't handle him being taken from me, too. He knew it."

"Fiona, there's no evide—"

"How could he survive that?" Fiona interrupted, her voice sounding shrill to her own ears.

"I get it. You don't want to hope. You'd rather think the worst, so you aren't let down when you get bad news. Believe me, I was an ER nurse. I completely get it. But you can't resign yourself to thinking that he's already gone."

"I have to. Because it's true. He's gone. It's only a matter of time before they find his body," Fiona whispered. "Who could survive that kind of explosion?"

"And then you allow yourself to deal with it. For now, you pray, okay? I understand. Besides being an ER nurse, I learned not long ago that my brother is a Navy SEAL. I couldn't let myself assume the worst when he didn't answer me. And it's just him and me. We lost our parents in a fire. Are you sure there isn't someone that can be here for you beside me?"

"I really want to call his mom. But I can't until I know more. She has some," she paused to find the right word without airing too much of Ransom's past that Angie—or Jon for that matter—might not know, "issues. I'm scared that if I call her too soon, she'll do something she shouldn't. I don't want to worry his sisters, either. I don't know if I have their correct numbers, anyway. But I can't risk them reaching out to his mom without more information."

"What about your parents?"

"They're several hours away. I don't want to tell anyone until I know more," she said instead of trying to explain their situation right now.

"Alright, then it's you and me until we hear something," Angie said. "As an aside, I know Jon just talked to Mac and Steven. Both are on their way here. I don't know how much you know, but Ransom is a part owner in Liaisons."

"I know," Fiona whispered.

"And do you know about the issues at Liaisons before the renovation happened?"

Fiona nodded. "Some."

"Fiona, it's possible what happened today has something to do with that," Angie softly said.

"How?"

"It isn't my place to say, but I know the guys met today at Liaisons. Something else happened."

"What?" Fiona demanded, straightening in the chair.

"Why don't we wait for Mac and Steven to get here?" Jon said from behind them. "Let's move to another room where there are less distractions."

21

Seated in what was clearly a conference room, still wrapped in her blanket with a fresh cup of non-alcohol laced coffee in front of her, Fiona listened. She knew a little about Angie's shooting, the murder of someone named Mandy, the fire at Liaisons that almost killed Nicole, and the missing money that Nicole discovered. She listened as the three men explained everything in a little more detail than Ransom had. And in truth, she hadn't asked a lot of questions before. She believed they had more time to do that. The three men around the table then added what they had discussed today. Someone destroyed room four. The room where the four of them, and they admitted who knew how many others might have, engaged in group sex. Fiona's jaw hit the floor when they disclosed that one of those women was Angie.

Fiona shot a look at Nicole, who had arrived earlier with Steven.

"It's okay. I'm over it," Nicole said with a wave of her hand. "It was before we were together. I just didn't appreciate learning about it through a third party."

Fiona could only imagine and really wanted to know when Nicole had found out about it.

"So now you see why we're concerned about Ransom's boat exploding," Mac said.

"Yes and no," Fiona admitted. "Why kill Ransom over it?"

"I don't know. The other two situations tried to take out the people we cared about," Steven said. "Whoever this is might have concluded it was better to take one of the four of us out instead. How long has Ransom had the boat and kept it at that marina?"

"He's had that boat since the endorsements he earned after the second Olympic games he competed in. That year's games were one of his best showings; he earned a lot more endorsements. How long he's been at that marina, I can't say. I know it was at a different marina before," she admitted, "but which one, I don't know. He sent me the directions today and all I could remember was that wasn't where we went in the past."

"Did he tell you about us confronting him today?"

"No. I hadn't spoken to him outside of text messages. Why?"

"Because the person who ruined the playroom at Liaisons has your height, build, and hair color. But," Jon said when Fiona started to defend herself, "she has tattoos that Ransom said you didn't have. We all can clearly see that you don't have at least one of them."

"I have no tattoos," she stated.

"None on your right wrist," Mac said, "and we can assume none on your left ankle."

Angie said, "None on the left ankle. I cleaned and bandaged some abrasions on her knees."

"We, the three of us men, would like to apologize to you. Even though you didn't know it, it certainly looked like you in the surveillance footage," Jon said. "I would like to show it to you if you think you could handle it right now."

"I want to see it more than you know," Fiona said, and meant it. She needed something else to focus on besides Ransom's death. And if she could help identify who might have killed him, she was all for it.

Jon grabbed a tablet, and after some tapping on the touch screen, the huge TV on the other side of the conference table came to life.

"This is the footage of the person and only the person earlier today at Liaisons. I understand Ransom told you about the recording abilities of Liaisons?" Jon said, but the statement sounded more like a question.

"Yes," she said. "He did while we were looking at the rooms that day at Liaisons."

"Can I ask a question first?" Steven interjected.

"Of course," Fiona said.

"Did you see Ransom's code for the backdoor?"

"I saw him punching something in, but never actually saw the numbers. By the time I realized what he was doing, he had unlocked the door."

Steven smiled. "I owe him another apology."

"Wait," Fiona said, suddenly putting two and two together and getting four, "you thought I got into the club?"

"Watch," Mac said, "and you'll see why."

Fiona did. She saw a figure sharing her same height and build enter through the back door she and Ransom had that day he took her to Liaisons. Then she spotted the small bit of hair that bore a resemblance to hers.

"Stop!" she asked. "How could someone have my hair color?"

"Hair color isn't entirely unique," Jon said.

"Mine is. I'm a natural orange red head. My natural color acts as a highlight. The browns and darker red shades are all salon created."

"Really?" Angie asked, studying Fiona's hair.

"Yes," Fiona said, picking up her phone and scrolling through her pictures. She had a picture of herself during those first Olympic games when she was still a carrot top. Opening the picture, she flipped the phone around to show the others around the table. "What looks natural now was not always the case."

"Damn it!" Jon said. "This adds just one more element to the scenario if that's the case because that person you see there—"

"Has my exact hair color that isn't natural," Fiona finished. "Play the rest of the video, please."

Jon did, but added, "I want to know where your hair salon is."

"Not in Charleston, anymore anyway," Fiona continued to watch the video footage and the person destroying the room. "The woman who first suggested the color could still be working. She used to work at a place in Summerville. When I left Charleston, she gave me the formulas for the other colors she added. I take it to whatever salon is in the area I'm living in."

When the video ended, she asked, "Why would I do something like that?"

"That was our question earlier today. Of course, we thought you'd seen his code and..." Mac's voice faded.

"That I was upset about what he told me he'd done in that room? We weren't together then. Sure, he and I would have had a lot of things to talk about regarding his activities at Liaisons. But I wouldn't have retaliated that way," she said.

"We know that now. Besides, Ransom spotted that whoever that woman was, she had tattoos. We confirmed that you don't. Which leaves us with many more questions than answers," Jon said.

22

———

"Are you sure you want to be alone?" Angie asked, turning to face Fiona, who was sitting in the back seat of Jon's car.

"Yes," Fiona said as she unbuckled her seatbelt. Angie and Jon had driven her back to her apartment. She really wanted to go to Ransom's house, but she no longer had a key and was sure he moved the hidden key she used to know about.

"I can take you to Ransom's place," Jon said from the driver's seat.

"I can't get in," Fiona said.

"From the little I know about Ransom, he likely has a hide-a-key outside," Jon said.

"I know he used to, but I doubt it's in the same place," Fiona said.

"It probably is. Buckle your seatbelt back. I'd rather leave you there than here right now," Jon said.

"You don't think there's any danger at his place?" Fiona asked.

"Doubt it. To put myself in the other person's shoes, I think they're sure they took care of the problem and you'll be safer at his place than yours."

Fiona fastened her seatbelt again. "Then take me there."

Jon said, "Angie, trade places with me. Let me make some calls," he said. Once they'd traded places, Jon put Ransom's address into the navigation system of the car. As they drove through the night, Jon made several calls.

When they reached Ransom's house, there were two SUVs parked out front and four men swarming the property. She only wondered what the neighbor's thought if they were paying any attention to what was happening outside. A quick glance at the homes showed dark windows. She felt sure the action had gone unnoticed.

"What's going on?" Fiona asked.

"I called some of my guys in to do a sweep of the place and make sure things were good. They found the key in a fake rock by the front door."

Fiona laughed.

When Jon shot her a questioning glance, she said, "It's still in the same place."

He shook his head and mumbled something to the effect of needing to change up a routine once in a while.

Once the three of them stood in the living room, Fiona said, "My car is still at the marina."

"Give me the keys. I'll have one of the guys bring it here. The next question is, do you want to be alone? I would feel better if we stayed with you," Jon said.

Fiona debated. She really wanted to be alone in Ransom's house. It would be her last goodbye to him.

"No. I want to be alone," she admitted.

"And while I think this is a safer place, I want to leave security in place. Despite what I said, I got to thinking and I wouldn't put it past the person behind this knowing you're here and taking things one step further if, for some reason, you're a target. We can't dismiss that possibility yet. You were meeting him at the boat."

"I appreciate your offer," Fiona said, "but I want to be alone. Besides, I don't think I was the target at all. They had no way of knowing that I was going to meet him there."

"If they hacked his phone, yes, they would," Jon argued.

"And if they did that, it wasn't to look for information on me," Fiona countered. "Ran was the target here, not me. And you can hack a phone?"

"I have," he confessed. "I'll leave some guys in the area. Two can go get your car. But I want eyes on this place while you're here."

"They can wait in the car," Fiona said.

"No," Jon argued. "There are too many bushes out back. One man out front and one out back. Otherwise, you come back with me and Angie to our place where there's an extra bedroom, which I don't think you have at your apartment."

Fiona debated. She needed to mourn, and she be unable to do that while others were in the house.

"They have to remain outside."

"They will," Jon said. "One team will get your car and bring you the keys. However, as long as you're here, there will be at least two people watching at all times."

"Fine," Fiona said.

After she handed her keys to Jon, she lingered in the living room, studying Ransom's furniture. She wished she had a glass of wine.

She pulled her phone from her purse, which somehow stayed with her throughout the entire ordeal, and texted Jon.

Fiona: I could use a glass of wine. Ransom doesn't keep alcohol in the house.

Jon's answer came back immediately.

Jon Vargas: I'll have them bring some to you with your car.

Fiona: Thanks.

Jon Vargas: The least I could do.

Fiona moved to the kitchen and grabbed a glass to fill with water while she waited. Ten minutes later, there was a knock at the front door.

"Ms. Campbell. This is Tank. I have your car keys and some wine."

She unlocked the door to find a man who embodied the name of Tank standing there holding her keys in one hand and a canvas tote with six bottles of wine in it in the other.

"Why are there six bottles of wine?"

"Jon didn't give me any direction except to get you some wine," he said, extending his hands to her. "I didn't know what you'd prefer, so there are a variety of types. There's a corkscrew in there too. I figured if he didn't have wine, he probably didn't have one of those either."

"Thank you, Tank," she said.

"I'll be out front for the next four hours. Ray is in the back. We'll change shifts every four hours. Jon will let you know who the next ones are. Don't open the door unless the name matches what he sends you, okay?"

"Yes," she said, taking the bag and her keys, "but I don't think I'll be answering anytime soon, should anyone knock."

"That's a good idea. Good night," Tank said and turned away.

Fiona shut and relocked the door before moving to the kitchen to unpack the wine. It was a wide variety of white and red—she wasn't picky about her wine. She had yet to meet a varietal she didn't like. She put the white wines in the refrigerator before she uncorked one bottle of red. Then she searched Ransom's cabinets for a wine glass. Finally, discovering one hidden in the back depths of a cabinet, she poured a generous glass and then went back and sat on the couch.

One glass of wine and an hour later, her eyelids were heavy. After jerking awake when her head bobbed, she rose from the couch and took her glass to the kitchen. She grabbed the water glass she filled earlier and wandered down the hall to Ransom's bedroom.

Realizing she had nothing of her own there, she used his bar of soap to wash her face—cringing the entire time as she missed her facial routine—then used his toothbrush to brush her teeth.

Afterwards, she dug through a drawer, found a t-shirt and pulled it on after removing all her clothing but her panties and crawled into his bed.

It smelled like him. She rolled to the center of the bed, where her head rested between two pillows. Then she shifted and grabbed his pillow in her arms. As she drifted off to sleep, she cuddled his pillow—which still smelled like him—and imagined Ransom holding her close as he did so often in this bed. They both honestly loved to cuddle as they fell asleep and would often wake up in the same position.

As the tears fell, she rolled over and hugged her own pillow instead. He would never hold her again. She would never wake up next to him. She would never see the heavy-lidded gaze he gave her in the morning.

Fiona cried herself to sleep. She grieved for Ransom and the life they never had, the baby she lost that would have linked them forever, and the fact that obviously she could never have her own happily ever after.

Ransom appeared in her dreams. She would only ever have him with her in her dreams. His hands pushing her away and then pulling her close when her hand wrapped around the part of him that always responded to her touch. He rolled onto his back. She straddled him and released his rapidly growing erection. Her hands skated over his toned chest and stomach. Her memory supplying every inch of him to her. She brought her mouth down to kiss him. Then he rolled them until he was on top. His lips were on hers; his hands skated over her body in a way she would never, ever forget. The soft strokes awakened desire, and she reveled in the sensations. She felt him in every way possible. It was one of the most erotic dreams she had ever had. She sighed when he entered her. She whispered, "I love you." She inwardly smiled at his groan of pleasure and soft words he spoke that she couldn't make out. His thrusts were long and languid, something they had rarely experienced together. Afterwards, he held her tight against him—her head pillowed on his chest.

She murmured, "How can I live without you?"

He whispered something she still couldn't interpret, and she fell into a deeper stage of sleep.

Knowing he would be there, with her, forever in her dreams. "Promise me you'll be here every night in my dreams."

23

―――

Ransom could barely believe he was alive. He didn't expect to find Fiona in his bed. But he held her tight against him after their lovemaking. His aching body wasn't what kept him awake. It was that he had believed that Fiona was awake when they made love. Instead, he now realized that she was sound asleep and had thought she was dreaming. He had to wake her.

He stretched and turned on the small bedside lamp. Her arms automatically tightened around him, preventing him from moving.

"Fi," he said and gently placed a kiss against her head. "Fi, sweetheart, wake up."

"I need a few minutes before we go again," she mumbled.

"Fiona," he said as he moved one arm so he could grasp her shoulder and gently shake her. "Wake up."

"You're so demanding. That's how I know this is a dream. Fine, but you'd better make it worth my time," she said while her hand skated down his stomach.

He seized her hand before it contacted his groin.

"Damn it, Fi, wake up," he snapped.

She froze in his arms and jerked her hand back from his grip. Then she sat up in bed, pulling away from his arms, clutching the sheet to her chest. "Ransom?"

He met her shocked gaze. She was awake now.

"Hey," he said and smiled.

"Hey? That's all you have to say to me. Hey?" she asked, her tone incredulous. "How are you alive? How did you get here?" she asked. Then her eyes widened. "Did we just have sex?"

"You were pretty insistent when I tried to wake you up," he said.

She lunged at him, and he caught her. He didn't know what to expect, but he certainly hadn't anticipated the soft thuds of her fists against his chest. "You scared me! How are you alive? Where have you been? What time is it?"

He wrapped his arms around her to halt the pounding of her fists. She wasn't really hurting him, but he was sore from the blast and swimming around until he could find a safe place to get out of the water; the time with emergency personnel had emotionally drained him.

"Stop," he whispered. "Shhh," he said, softly stroking her hair when he realized she was crying.

"How?" she sobbed.

"I'm a swimmer, remember. But I had to swim a good bit to get away from the flames, oil, gas, and whatever else was in the water. I tried to call, but you didn't answer. And it's close to three in the morning."

"My phone didn't ring," she said and tried to pull away.

"You can check it in a minute. Let me hold you. For a moment I thought I'd never get to hold you again."

Her arms tightened around his neck. "I didn't think I'd ever hold you again. Tell me what happened?"

"I'm too tired right now. I will tell you, but can we just sleep for a bit?"

"Why didn't anyone call me?"

"We all tried. You didn't answer any phone calls or texts," he said.

This time, when she tried to pull from his embrace, he let her. He knew she had to check and see why she hadn't heard her phone.

"Wow," she said. Her phone screen lit up the room. Then she turned the phone to check the side. "My ringer is off. That's odd. I wouldn't have done that because I was waiting to hear about you."

"It was probably an accident. My mom's phone does it a lot when it's in her purse. I think it's because of where she puts it. Speaking of Mom, does she know?"

"No. I was waiting to tell them until I had something more to say than your boat blew up and you were dead," she said as she returned her phone to the nightstand.

She snuggled back in his arms and rested her head on his chest again. He held her tightly.

"Can we get just a few hours of sleep? I'll tell you everything after that. The others are coming by at noon."

"Did you see them?" she questioned while yawning.

"No, I only spoke to them on the phone. Now go back to sleep," he said before he kissed the top of her head. "I need to sleep."

It was the last thing he remembered saying to her before sleep claimed him.

24

The obnoxious sound of an alarm clock woke Ransom. Letting go of Fiona, he rolled and stifled a groan that was the automatic response to his sore muscles. He picked up his phone and muted the alarm. He had set it for ten o'clock as soon as he got home last night. He knew he would be slow getting up and would need some time to collect his thoughts before everyone arrived. A long, hot shower wouldn't hurt. When he'd reached home in the early hours, he used the pool shower to wash off the ocean water and whatever else had clung to him before he went into the house and discovered Fiona in his bed.

Now a long, hot shower sounded like heaven. He stole a quick glance at Fiona and saw she was still sound asleep. He rose from the bed and strolled to the kitchen to fix a cup of coffee. As he waited for it to brew, he saw the bottle of wine sitting on the counter next to a bag with two others still in it. When he opened the refrigerator to take out the bottle of creamer, he saw three more bottles. Apparently, Fiona had decided to stay a while when she thought he was dead. He made a mental note to make sure they went with her when she returned to her apartment later. He didn't need them here.

"Hey."

He glanced over his shoulder to see Fiona approaching him wearing one of his t-shirts. He knew she had worn it last night when he joined her in bed. However, he had taken it off during their lovemaking, and she had spent the rest of the night naked.

"Hey. Coffee?"

"Yes," she said. "And I'm sorry the wine is here. I know you don't keep that in the house. But I wanted a glass last night while I grieved for you."

"A glass? There are six bottles, Fiona."

"Blame Jon or Tank or whoever picked them up. Speaking of which, they were supposed to be watching over the house."

"Remember last night I told you I talked to Jon?" he asked. When she nodded, he continued, "Jon told them I was on my way home. They're still out there. Jon was worried whoever did this could know that I survived."

"What happened?"

"Like I said last night, let's wait for the others. I went through it enough last night with the police and emergency workers."

"Not Jon?"

"No. If the police told him, that's their business. I talked to Steven and Mac for a minute, too. That's why they're all gathering here later."

"I see. So why are you up already? It's only ten."

"I want a long, hot shower. Last night I used the pool shower. I was too tired to do anything more."

"I'm going to go home to change while you do that. Do you want me to bring anything back for lunch?"

"That would be a help. I thought about ordering some pizzas."

"I'll grab something. I'll text Nicole too. I vaguely remember something about a food allergy with her."

"Take the wine with you, please."

"Of course," she smiled. "I'm sorry. I know your rule."

"It's just too tempting of a habit to fall into."

She moved into his space and gently wrapped her arms around his waist. "I know."

He circled her with his arms. "Thank you."

She lifted her eyes to him and smiled. "Kiss me quick."

He did, and then she slipped from his embrace and went back down the hall to the bedroom.

He finished making his cup of coffee and was walking back down the hall when she met him in the hallway. "I'll be back shortly."

"Okay," he said, leaning in to kiss her again.

Then she was gone, and he was alone in his bedroom, gazing at the bed they had shared the night before as he sipped from the mug. He smiled at the memory of trying to wake her when he first discovered she was in his bed. She was so insistent on making love to him. Of course, she'd been dreaming. What caused him to smile was she told him she loved him. It was the first time she had said it since the big fight.

Walking to the bathroom, he placed his coffee cup on the counter and studied his reflection in the mirror. He had a solid two-day growth of beard, but decided he didn't have the energy to shave. He was about a week overdue for a haircut, but again, nothing he could do about it now. He'd take care of that tomorrow.

He lifted his shirt and removed it; thankful Fiona had been unable to see the bruising on his body. The blast had knocked the air out of him and when he hit the water, several pieces of the boat came down on him. He believed it was fortunate that he had only blacked out for what he judged to be seconds. The only reason he thought it was such a brief amount of time was because of what he remembered catching sight of just before he hit the water and what he noticed when he came to. He was aware of the second explosion, which also hurled debris at him that caused more bruising. That was when he went under and swam away from the marina, and the gas and oil in the water. When he resurfaced is when he heard the last explosion. His mind figured it was some kind of terrorist attack but couldn't figure out why they would target private boats and a marina not used by the military—at least to his knowledge.

He dropped the shirt on the counter and then moved to remove the loose shorts he had tugged on earlier. He needed that shower. Hell, he wanted to go soak in the hot tub, but there wasn't enough time, and he didn't want Fiona to see the bruises. Instead, he stretched his hand into the shower stall and turned the water on and set the temperature control to scalding. While he waited for the water to warm—it always took longer than he wanted—he used the bathroom.

Once in the shower under the spray, he dialed the temperature back just a little. The tank would empty too soon if he left it that hot. As he stood and let the water release some of the tension in his muscles, he considered putting in one of the on-demand water heaters. When he did the renovation, the contractor had suggested it, but Ransom hadn't wanted to do much more than the structural stuff in the living area. Now, as he stood there letting the water massage his shoulders and back, he considered gutting the bathroom. He knew kitchen and bathroom updates sold a house—not that he had any intention of selling it soon. He hoped Fiona would move in with him.

Grabbing the bar of soap, he thought about Fiona as he created a foaming pile of suds in his hands and scrubbed. Would she move in with him? Hell, they'd barely even been able to talk about where they wanted things to go. Sure, they'd slept together the past week since they agreed to be together again. Which was so weird. In the past, they never really had to say they were together or not. It was just a fact. It was strange that this time they actually used words to define their relationship. They were back together. The question now was where did they want it to go? His life was in Charleston. Her life was...he realized he didn't know where her parents were now. Maybe they would move back to Charleston if she did. Fiona had been born and raised in Charleston until they moved a few years before the first Olympic Games they'd been in. They moved back after that and stayed until Fiona started college. She had gone to the University of West Virginia, and they followed her there. When she came back to Charleston, the last time they dated, her parents hadn't moved back. But he couldn't remember where they were. He rinsed his body and stepped from the shower.

As he dried off, he heard a phone ringing. It wasn't the ringtone of his phone though—he'd lost his in yesterday's chaos. Wrapping the towel around his waist just in case he was no longer alone in the house, he followed the ringing to discover it was Fiona's phone. Apparently, she'd forgot it when she left earlier.

He studied the name on the caller id. It said Mom or Dad. Well, hell, he was just thinking about them.

"Hello?" he said when he answered the call, expecting to hear one of their voices.

"Oh, is Ms. Campbell there?"

"I'm sorry she isn't," he said to the strange female voice. He knew it wasn't her mother's voice.

"This is her number, though?"

"It is. She left her phone here when she went to take care of something. Can I help you?"

"Who are you?"

"Montgomery Ransom," he said.

Before he could say more, the voice said, "Oh. Mr. Ransom, you're on the emergency contact list."

"Excuse me? Has something happened to Fiona's parents?"

"Ran! I'm back. Where are you?" Fiona called just before she walked into the bedroom. "There you are..."

"Please hold, she just walked back in," Ransom said. He moved towards her, hand on the mouthpiece, and told her, "You have a phone call. It's about your parents."

Her eyes widened as she looked at his bruised torso. He watched her stiffen as his words registered, and then she practically snatched the phone from his fingers. She turned away, but Ransom stopped her by grabbing her shoulders and holding her in place. He hit the speaker button on the phone before she could raise it to her ear. He was going to hear this conversation. Fi would need his help to get through it if something had happened to them.

"He...hel...hello?" Fiona finally managed to say.

"Ms. Campbell. This is Shirley, the social worker at Harboring Pines. There's been an incident."

He watched as Fiona bowed her head. "What's happened?"

"Well, as you know, we've placed your parents on opposite sides of the facility because of how they bicker and fight. Your father was having one of his good days this morning and wanted to see your mother. He somehow reached the unit your mother was on and noticed her sitting in the common area talking to another resident. They were holding hands. Your father didn't take that too well and when he neared them, your mother threw a cup of water at him and accused him of stalking her. Your father lost his footing and fell. He broke his elbow when he landed."

Fiona massaged her forehead with her free hand.

What in the hell was going on? Facility? Bickering?

"Okay. Do I need to come?"

"No, they transported your father to the hospital, and they administered a light sedative to your mother. Who is now resting."

"How can we prevent this from happening again?"

"We could move one of them to another facility," Shirley said.

"There isn't one with your skills or ratings anywhere close by. It would be so much harder for me to visit them at two separate facilities."

"I understand; but Ms. Campbell, they aren't doing well here. It's difficult to make sure when they have a good day, they don't go looking for the other."

"I understand. Do what needs to be done. I can pay for another person to sit with one of them more often to prevent that."

"When are you returning to town?"

"It wasn't supposed to be for another two months, but I can make a trip sooner. I have some things to take care of while there. I'll let you know," Fiona said, her tone sounding defeated.

"Thank you, Ms. Campbell. Is there anything I can do to help?"

"Could you research facilities near Charleston, South Carolina?"

Ransom squeezed her shoulders. Judging from the conversation, there was something very wrong with her parents. When she cast a quick glance at him, he gave her a reassuring smile and gently kissed her temple.

"I can do that. For just one of them?"

"No, both."

"Okay," Shirley said.

"Goodbye," Fiona said and when Shirley echoed the same, Fiona ended the call. After several seconds of standing there, she turned to face him. His arms slipped from where his hands had rested on her shoulders and moved down to wrap loosely around her waist. Without taking her gaze from his chest, she softly said, "Mom and Dad are in a memory care facility. They have been for about a year now."

"Why didn't you tell me?" Ransom asked, tightening his arms, pressing her body into full contact with his. He fought against the impulse to make her look him in the eye.

"I've barely accepted the fact that my parents, despite still living, are gone for me. To them, I'm a teenager or in my early twenties. They don't recognize each other and bicker like school children with crushes on each other."

Ransom laid his cheek against the top of her head when she leaned against his bare chest. She had been through so much since she last left him. "That's why they don't know about Hope, isn't it?" Ransom remembered her mentioning that she hadn't told her parents.

"Yes," she whispered.

"Why am I listed as an emergency contact, Fi?"

She let out a deep breath as she said, "Because I knew if something happened to me, you'd make sure they were okay, even if we weren't together. You loved them and they loved you. You still look more or less the same in the face, so they should recognize you."

"Why don't they recognize you? You don't look all that different, Fi."

"I think it's because I look more like an adult compared to what they remember. I can't talk about this anymore right now," she said, shaking her head.

"Later then," he said. Even though he had more questions, he'd honor her request of postponing it until after their conversation with the others.

Then he regretted the decision when she asked, "Do they hurt?"

"Does what hurt?"

"The bruises." She raised her head to look him in the eye and said, "Last night, you downplayed how badly your injuries were."

He held her eyes with his. "No," he whispered, "they don't hurt. They just look awful."

"I picked up food and was heading back here," she said, changing the subject. "I was looking for my phone to call you and tell you that, but then I couldn't find it. Then I realized that after I called Nicole and she told me what I wanted to know, I laid the phone down as I got dressed."

"What did you need to ask Nicole?" Ransom asked, letting her go and moving to his closet to get dressed.

"I remembered her saying something about a food allergy that first night I met her, but I couldn't remember what it was."

"What is it?" he asked, yanking a button-down shirt off a hanger and reaching for a pair of jeans.

"She's allergic to tomatoes."

"Really? I don't think I've ever met anyone allergic to tomatoes."

"It's rare, but it happens, according to her."

"So, what did you get for us to eat? Certainly not pizza."

"She suggested a deli she frequently gets sandwiches from. She told me what she gets and to let them know it's for her and they'll be extra sure to avoid the tomatoes. Then she just offered to call it in. I made it easy and told her to get everyone a club sandwich without tomatoes. There are some in a container, though, if you want to add them. They also had jugs of tea and lemonade. Oh, and I got some of their homemade chips."

"You weren't gone that long, Fi."

"Didn't you hear me say that Nicole called it in? They were just about done with it when I got there. Easy peasy. Now finish getting dressed," she said and left the bedroom.

Ransom headed to the dresser to grab a pair of underwear. He was debating about socks when he heard the doorbell ring. Socks could wait, he would wear flip-flops.

He quickly dressed, ran a comb through his hair, and then joined Fiona and the others in the dining area. So far, only Steven and Nicole had arrived. Nicole was helping Fiona set up the sandwiches on a platter and the chips in a serving bowl. To make things easy, he grabbed a large tub and filled it with some ice from a bag he kept in the freezer for times like this. He then stuck the jugs of tea and lemonade into the ice. After setting that on the counter near the platters of food, he rummaged around for the disposable cups he thought he had stashed away. After searching every cabinet and coming up empty, he went to the cabinet where he stored the glasses and retrieved seven and set them on the counter.

As he did that, Mac arrived, followed by Jon and Angie.

"Let's fix plates and then I'll explain," Ransom said.

No one disagreed and quickly helped themselves to the food and sat at the table.

Ransom fixed a plate after everyone else had and then took the empty seat next to Fiona.

"We can wait until after you eat," Fiona said. Angie quickly agreed. While they ate, they chatted about the weather, sports, and finally, weekend plans.

"What happened?" Jon asked when Ransom finished the last chip on the plate.

"I left Liaisons and decided that after our meeting, I could use a day out on the water. I texted Fiona on my way over."

"When was the last time you went out on the boat?" Steven asked.

"It's been a few weeks. The last time was the weekend Fiona went to a competition with her athlete. I was checking over things while I waited for her to arrive. I had just bent over to look at the engine and noticed a wire that I didn't remember seeing before."

"Is that when I arrived?" Fiona asked.

Ransom nodded. "I didn't have time to check it. One minute I'm standing there watching her walk towards me and the next I was flying through the air. I know I was unconscious for a few seconds. I don't remember hitting the water. To make a long story short, I swam away from the marina to get away from the oil, gas, and debris. I had to swim a good way out. As I was searching for someplace safe to come back in, the Coast Guard found me. Naturally, they had questions. Especially after I told them I had been at the marina."

"When did you change marinas?" Fiona asked.

"I moved to Charleston Harbor when a slip came available last year. It's closer to the house, too. But because of its location, the Yorktown parked next to it, and I didn't know if other boats would pay attention to a person in the water. I had to swim around Patriots Point. It's a good thing I still swim laps daily."

"So, how long did the Coast Guard question you?" Mac said.

"A good hour as they transported me to the Coast Guard station in downtown Charleston. Then they called Charleston PD, which naturally wasn't easy to deal with considering the situation. They badgered me for a good hour. Finally, one officer agreed to take me to the marina. When we got there, the first responders were still there and said that I had missed Fiona's departure by nearly two hours. I didn't have my phone; it's either in pieces or at the bottom of the harbor."

"How long did they question you at the marina before they called me?" Jon asked.

"Another hour," Ransom groaned. "Exhaustion was sinking in by that point. They believed I knew more than I actually did. What is it with the police and us lately? Why in the hell would I blow up my own boat, much less how many others?"

"Insurance money?" Steven said.

Ransom snorted in response.

"They still hold a grudge against me for the corruption fallout a few months back," Jon said. "I have a feeling there's still some housecleaning to be done. But this was a different jurisdiction than we've dealt with before."

Everyone fell silent.

"So how did you get home?" Fiona finally asked.

"First, they took me to the hospital to get examined. That took another three hours. That was when I tried to call you but got no answer. Finally, they released me, and they were kind enough to call me a cab," Ransom replied.

"Why did you come home instead of going to my place?" Fiona asked.

"At that point, I was just exhausted," Ransom said. "I knew you'd see the messages and missed calls and would follow up when you woke up."

"Why didn't you have your guys wake me up?" Fiona inquired of Jon. "They, and you, knew I was here."

"I didn't have time," Jon said. "I was dealing with phone calls and further questions from authorities about why I was involved in the situation. Which leads me back to the idea that the different precincts talk and that they watch each other's backs. By the time I could reach them directly, Ransom was already home. I told them to answer to no one but me."

"Why?" Steven asked.

"I'm troubled by the fact that Maverick still hasn't discovered who was using my login information at RLS."

"You don't think it was Maverick, do you?" Mac asked.

"No," Jon said, shaking his head at the same time. "Maverick has something going on, but it definitely isn't that."

"What do you mean?" Angie asked.

"He's been secretive lately. And I still can't forget that someone notified him the night you had to tend to his injuries. I'm running a new background check on him, but I know he wouldn't betray me. We've been through too much together."

"Okay, let's refocus. We can circle back to that later. Did they know anything about what happened?" Ransom asked.

"No," Jon answered. "The news this morning reported five boats in pieces, at least another ten with fire, smoke, or water damage."

"How does a boat get water damage?" Nicole asked.

"Fire hoses pump a lot of water. Some boats near those on fire were likely soaked and that could cause some issues. They might not see it right away, though."

"What now?" Fiona asked.

"We wait. Maverick is working this for me," Jon said.

"And you're sure we can trust him?" Ransom asked.

"I'd trust him with my life," Jon said.

"Okay. We wait. In the meantime," Nicole said, "I have some work to get back to."

"Yes, I have a book to finish," Steven said.

"And I know we have a mountain of details to work through. Like setting a wedding date," Angie said.

"We'll help clean up," Mac said.

"No," Fiona said. "I've got it."

Once the others left, Ransom took care of cleaning up the dishes while Fiona stored away the remaining food.

"So, what do you want to do now?" Ransom asked. He could use a nap, to be completely honest.

"I think I'd like to see Liaisons," Fiona said.

Ransom couldn't hold back his surprise. "Really?"

"Yes. I'd like to see it with people in it and how they interact."

"Don't you have to be with your athlete?"

"Tomorrow afternoon. Luckily, today, after dealing with everything yesterday and last night, was a day off."

"Can I take a quick nap first? Besides, this time of day, it is usually pretty slow at the club. It's still working hours for most people."

"Oh. Okay. Yes, take a nap."

"What will you do while I nap?" Ransom asked, wrapping his arms around her waist and pulling her close.

"I'm going to do some research."

"Research on what?"

"A realtor to sell Mom and Dad's house. Look at what to do with the stuff still in it. Find a place for me here."

"Want some help with that?"

She shook her head. "Go take a nap. It's something I think I need to do alone."

"You'll wake me up if you need me?"

"If I need you, yes," she said, looking at his chest.

"Fi," he said as his right hand shifted from her waist and lifted her chin, so she would look him in the eye. "Promise me. I'm here for you."

"I know," she said, tears filling her eyes.

"Baby," he groaned as he rested his forehead against hers. He hated that she was dealing with something he was unable to fix for her.

"It's nothing. Just everything the past few days is catching up with me," she said with a teary smile.

"Could it wait one more day?" he asked.

"I suppose," she said.

"Then we'll deal with it tomorrow," he said, raising his head. "Come, take a nap with me."

25

"Allison spent hours in that room and didn't find a single fingerprint," Maverick said. "I've added the recent issues to the presentation to see if it can help with what might be occurring."

"How is that possible?" Nicole asked.

"Several reasons, actually," Maverick said. "Here, look at this." A document popped up on the giant screen in the RLS conference room.

Ransom examined the document. When he was unable to figure out what he was looking at, he demanded, "What is this?"

"It's a list of reasons someone might not have fingerprints."

"What?" Angie, Fiona, and Mac asked simultaneously.

"There are several medical conditions that could lead to the absence of identifiable fingerprints, but also, and I learned this from my research, part of what leaves a print is sweat. So many of these people also might have missing sweat glands in their hands, leading to the absence of fingerprints."

"What about smudges?" Jon asked.

"People who work extensively with their hands can form calluses that smooth away the markers used in fingerprinting. Leading to smudges rather than actual prints," Maverick said.

"How common are these diseases?" Steven asked.

"Rare. Extremely rare," Maverick said, "but we aren't excluding someone who might have purposely eliminated their prints for one reason or another."

"You're saying there's no way to identify her?" Fiona asked.

"At this point, yes. She didn't leave even one strand of hair. Not a drop of sweat, either. And she should have worked up a sweat based on the video I saw," Maverick said.

Ransom shook his head in disbelief. "I can't believe we aren't going to find out who it was. They're just going to get away with it."

"I'll keep digging," Maverick said. "In the meantime, we continue surveillance."

"Were any prints found in the room?" Fiona asked.

"Not a single one. But that isn't surprising given the rigorous cleaning standards we have. The cleaning staff wear gloves to protect themselves from the chemicals we're required by law to use and from, um, the other..."

"Bodily fluids?" Ransom offered, suppressing a laugh at Maverick's obvious discomfort in finding a word to describe things in a less vulgar manner in front of the women.

"Yes," Maverick said, "because of the gloves from the cleaning staff and the cleaning requirements of the playrooms, there wasn't a single print in that room. And before you ask, I had Allison print another room just to compare. She found a few prints on the inside of one bureau and nowhere else. And even those were partials or smudged beyond use because of how people often handle furniture."

"Which room did she print?" Jon asked.

"Room two. It's one of the most used rooms. We pulled the camera footage for the last week of that room as well. We didn't watch the footage, just counted how many times it dumped the recordings. In one week, that room had forty-three camera backups transferred to the long-term storage server."

"In one week? That room alone?" Fiona asked.

Maverick nodded.

That number didn't surprise Ransom, and he knew it was no surprise Steven, Jon, or Mac either. It probably sounded like a lot to Fiona, but in truth, divide that number by seven and it was about six times per day. Which in his mind wasn't a lot, considering some of those might be from when the room was being cleaned. Despite the instruction to put a marker on the door if the room was being cleaned, many members just walked into the room not registering the marker. When the four of them had assumed control of the club, they had directed the cleaning staff to lock the door while they were in the room. So, of those forty-three occurrences, and at just over six per day, in his mind, at least three a day were cleanings.

"Let's see the timeline. Don't talk us through it, just show it to us," Jon said.

Maverick minimized the document on the screen and opened the presentation with the timeline.

"Let me explain that the only reason I have used when Jon and Angie met is that it seemed to be a catalyst for some of this," Maverick said.

Mid-February—Jon and Angie meet

Late February—first round of notes arrives to Jon and Angie; Someone searches Angie's apartment

March—second round of notes arrive to Jon and Angie; Security breach at RLS and Jon's place

Late March—Jon, Steven, Mac, and Ransom make the first offer on Liaisons; multiple offers made for the next six weeks

Early April—Discovery of police corruption and cover up when looking into the murder of Maybel Preston

Mid-April—Carlotta shoots Angie at Liaisons; Previous owners accept the offer to sell Liaisons

Early May—Someone murders Mandy at Liaisons; Nicole discovers the missing money; Jon, Steven, Mac, and Ransom take over ownership of Liaisons

Mid-May—Discovery of missing documents; Nicole caught in the fire at Liaisons

Mid-July—Liaisons reopens; An unknown person vandalizes PR4 seven days after the club reopens; Ransom's boat explodes

"Regarding Ransom's boat," Maverick said, "I found one camera further away. Our Liaisons vandal was in the same area as the marina shortly before the explosion. I have her leaving, but the camera is too far away to see where she went or to get a good shot to do any facial recognition. Same hoodie and same small lock of hair on display."

"When you look at it like this, it certainly looks like someone is out to close Liaisons or take out the four of you," Nicole said. "Especially with Ransom's boat exploding."

"The lock of hair on display also could be someone trying to frame Fiona for something," Maverick murmured.

"It doesn't explain why someone tried to kill Nicole in that fire," Steven said.

"No, it doesn't. But I think the bigger question is why? We discussed so many different scenarios and none of them really make sense. Why go after the club or one of you? Why not just leave?" Angie asked. "Can't they still terminate their membership at any time? And I agree with Maverick. Why frame Fiona for something?"

"Yes, but I came to understand a long time ago that people in desperate need often do things that are illogical," Jon said. "The Fiona angle is a new one. Have you had any issues with stalkers in the past?"

Fiona shook her head. "No."

Ransom couldn't think of anyone who would want to frame Fiona for vandalism and whatever one called what happened to his boat and the marina.

"Have there been any offers to sell?" Maverick asked.

"No," Mac said, "or at least no one has reached out to me."

"Or me," Jon said.

"Nope," Steven said.

"Not a single word," Ransom said.

"Here are the suggested theories," Maverick said, displaying a different list on the screen.

THEORIES

Jealous spouse or lover

Jilted spouse or lover

Membership denied after visiting and possibly taking part in activities in Playroom 4

Declined time in Playroom 4 by R, J, M, and/or S or other members

Wants Liaisons closed for good or at least wants to own it

Grudge against R, J, M, and/or S

"Don't forget the rape accusation," Steven said. "My source says it's still an active case."

"I'll add it," Maverick said, making a note on the pad of paper in front of him.

"Can you tell us anything more about that?" Ransom asked.

Steven shook his head. "They're keeping it under tight wraps. The police corruption discovered back in April makes me uneasy, and it's possible that there's a connection to it. That made headlines and didn't look good for a lot of people. You know there were many people extremely angry about it."

"They aren't talking to me either," Jon said. "They cooperate with me when they have to for business, but if I ask about anything else, they shut their mouths."

"What about drugs?" Fiona asked.

Ransom said, "No drugs in the club."

"No," Fiona said, shaking her head. "Wasn't Carlotta the head of a cartel? Could this be them?"

"This isn't really their style," Jon said. "Cartels like to make a big statement. These are too small. Besides, they'd come after me, not Liaisons."

"But you own Liaisons now," Fiona argued. "That could hurt you financially."

"No," Ransom said before Jon could speak. "Remember, we don't make money from the club. The funds received guarantees its self-sufficiency."

"The cartel wouldn't know that," Fiona argued. "I still don't understand that. Why own it if it doesn't make you any money?"

Ransom opened his mouth to explain, but this time Mac beat him to it. "Because if our intention was to make money, we'd have to increase prices so much that the members wouldn't stay. Furthermore, we bought it because of our dissatisfaction with how it was being managed. Liaisons has supported itself for decades. In hindsight, we probably should have set it up so that the members have more of a say in the rules. But they never did before, so we left it as is."

"Is there any rumor about that?" Fiona asked. "That could be the reason behind it. Could there be members who are dissatisfied with how you're managing things and want to have a greater say in the rules? That doesn't sound too different from your reasons for buying it from the previous owners."

Ransom glanced at his business partners. They shook their heads. "At least not that we've heard of," Ransom said, "but it's another point to consider. We were never told if there were any other offers when we made ours. Could there be someone interested in buying the club from us and deciding if there were enough problems, we'd throw our hands up and spread the word we want out?"

"Wouldn't turn down the suggestion of it," Jon said. "Add it to the list, too," he said, shifting his gaze to face Maverick. "Is there anything else? I want to try dinner tonight at Liaisons."

"Not really," Maverick said.

"We'll join you," Ransom said as he stood. "Fiona has wanted to see Liaisons when it's open and we just haven't been able to. Might as well have dinner there, too."

26

———

"Why are we using the front entrance?" Fiona asked.

"Because I have to sign you in," Ransom said as he led her from the back of the building to the front through a narrow alley.

"We couldn't have entered from the rear and accomplished that?"

"Yes, but I'm sure people would have stopped us along the way. It's just easier this way. If we make you a member, we can have a little more leeway. As an owner, I rarely use the front door. The managers keep an eye on the camera on the back door and log us in when we come in. I understand Jon has them log him and Angie in that way."

"I see. How many times can I attend before I have to become a member?" Fiona asked, carefully navigating around a puddle.

"Three, but you get three more if you apply and are waiting for acceptance."

"I don't think I—"

"Fi," Ransom said, coming to a stop and facing her, "we have a couple of different alternatives. I can switch my membership to a couple's one. You'd still have to go through the application process though."

"Does that mean we can only come here together?"

"No, but it makes it more financially attractive to couples."

"Ran, I don't want you coming here without me," she said. "Well, I don't want you going into a playroom without me," she amended.

"Easily arranged, my love," Ransom said with a smile. "As an owner, I have to be here from time to time, but I promise you I won't enter a playroom without you for anything beyond club business."

"What does that mean?"

"Like when someone vandalized room four, I won't go into a playroom unless I'm with you or have a valid reason as an owner."

"Oh, okay," Fiona said. And she was okay with that. She trusted Ransom. Cheating on her wasn't one of her concerns. The issue was hers and hers alone. That never-ending fear of losing him was her problem, and she had to handle it. She had almost lost him in the explosion—she even thought she had. She had to deal with the fear and decided to seek a counselor to help her process through why she felt that way. She broke up with him that first time for reasons other than her fear of losing him. It was because they had both been so young and not truly ready for the commitment that was being talked about. The first boyfriend she had lost was during that breakup. Come to think of it, the second one was in there too. But she still remembered fearing she would lose Ransom and knew that she wouldn't have been capable of dealing with that. She vowed to herself to make an appointment with a counselor and work through it along with the inevitable loss of her parents.

Ransom held the door open, and she crossed the threshold into Liaisons. It looked different at night. The heavy curtains muted the light filtering to the street from the large windows. It added a level of mystery to the place.

"Good evening, Mr. Ransom," the man behind the desk greeted.

"Evening, Martin. And remember, just Ransom is fine. I need to sign in Ms. Campbell and if you could pull a membership packet for her to review, that would be great."

Fiona watched Ransom print and sign his name on a register, then printed hers, and handed over a pen. "Sign there," he said, pointing to the line next to where he had printed her name.

She did.

"Sign this," he said, placing a piece of paper in front of her.

"What's this?"

"A non-disclosure agreement," Ransom said.

She signed where he indicated and set the pen back in the holder and accepted a folder from the man behind the desk.

"Have a good evening, Martin," Ransom said and guided her away from the desk.

"You as well, sir."

"Do I need to put my purse somewhere?"

"We'll place it back in the office," he whispered. "Another perk of being an owner."

"Shouldn't the rules be the same for everyone?"

"They are. But as owners, we sometimes need to deal with urgent situations, which means we have to always be accessible. The members understand that if we have our phone out, it's because we are dealing with a problem and moving away from our current location. We have a few lock boxes in the office, which is where we leave our phones sometimes. Management knows we're here, and they can come get us rather than call. But we don't want to go out front to grab our phone if there is a problem. Also, there's a phone in the office with each of our cell phone numbers stored in it. We just have to press one button."

"Why aren't there phones in the playrooms?"

"There never have been. We debated the idea of something like a hotel phone but decided against it right now. If there's an emergency, there are protocols in place that must be followed. We can talk about that later, though. Come on," he said as he took her hand and led her through the door into the lounge.

She studied the quiet atmosphere. It was dark, but intimate and cozy. The soft light was everywhere and nowhere at the same time. A petite lamp adorned each table. Sunken lights illuminated pathways through tables and chairs, but the effect was so subdued that you almost felt like you were intruding on the occupants of the tables as they walked past.

"Where are we going?" she asked.

"See the booth straight ahead? That's where, and then I'll take the stuff back to the office once Jon and Angie arrive. I'm not leaving you alone out here."

"Why?" she asked as she stopped walking and turned to face him.

"Because every single guy in this place will pounce. Probably some women too. I'm not ready to deal with the green-eyed monster yet," he said.

"Seriously?"

"I couldn't be more serious if I tried," he said as he moved in front of her towing her along behind him.

As Fiona casually observed her surroundings. It surprised her to notice that people were paying attention to them. She could see interest in the eyes of some of them; others showed curiosity. She refocused her attention back to Ransom's shoulders.

They reached the booth, and he moved so she could slide in first. He then sat next to her.

"Jon and Angie shouldn't be too far behind us. I'm surprised they didn't make it before us, considering they would have just come in the back."

"There they are," she said, nodding toward the door that she knew led to the playrooms.

"We had to leave Angie's purse in the office," Jon said, sliding in.

"I was going to take Fiona's back there once you arrived. I'll be right back," he said, taking her purse and the membership packet with him.

As soon as he stepped away, a waiter came up to the table. "Are you all interested in dinner or drinks?"

"Yes, to both," Jon said. "Please leave the menus. Angie, what would you like to drink?"

They placed their drink orders, and the waiter left. Ransom returned to the table just as the drinks were being delivered.

"I didn't know if you wanted your usual or a double," Jon said.

Fiona glanced at Ransom. She knew he didn't drink at home and on occasion had a glass of wine with her at the Crimson Room or her apartment.

"Tell Tim to make me my usual, but make it a double," Ransom told the waiter.

"Sure thing."

As Jon and Angie perused the menu, Fiona leaned toward Ransom. "A double?"

He turned and whispered in her ear, "My usual is water in a rocks glass. If I ask for my usual but a double, it's vodka with a splash of water. Jon doesn't know what those words mean. He thinks it means I want a single or a double. And I never have over three drinks when I'm here if I'm drinking alcohol. That's my rule."

"Is it a double, though?" she murmured.

"No, it's one shot of vodka," he said and kissed her ear. "What do you want to eat?"

She took the menu and glanced at it. She found the selections on the menu to be limited, but everything sounded fantastic.

"I think I'd like a pork belly bowl," she said. "I'm in the mood for a little Asian cuisine tonight."

"That should go nicely with that rosé wine you're drinking. I think I'll try the chicken," Ransom said. "Will you share a bite with me?"

"Of course," she said, as she reviewed the description for the chicken and grew curious about the herbed risotto offered with it. "But only if you share too."

After they placed their orders, the four engaged in conversation while waiting for the food to arrive. Fiona joined the discussion but also watched what was happening around her. She saw a single man approach a woman and after some conversation they left for the back together.

What she didn't see, and was very thankful for it, was people engaging in sexual activity out in the open. She wasn't naïve enough to think that something wasn't happening in the darkness under the tables, but she couldn't see anything if it was happening. Truthfully, she'd expected some kind of—well, she didn't know what to call it—happening right out in the open.

"Not what you expected, is it?" Jon asked.

"No," Fiona agreed.

"Truthfully, my first time here surprised me, too," Angie said. "I imagined people walking around naked and engaging in sex right out here. Almost like dinner and a show," she said with a laugh. "Of course, the club didn't serve food then."

"Pretty much what I was expecting," Fiona laughed.

Ransom's hand rested on her thigh, drawing her attention back to him. When she looked at him, he just raised an eyebrow in question. She knew he was asking if she wanted to go into a playroom.

She stole a glance at Jon and Angie, who had their heads together talking.

She leaned closer to Ransom. "Just us, though."

He smiled. "I never assumed otherwise. I'll be back."

Fiona watched him walk into the back.

"I think we're going to head home," Angie said. "I have an early meeting tomorrow with a wedding planner."

"It was nice having dinner with you both," Fiona said.

"It was. We'll wait for Ransom to get back," Jon said. "I know he wouldn't thank me for leaving you here alone with so many people looking for someone to occupy some time with."

Ransom neared the table on the tail end of Jon's sentence.

"Thank you for keeping an eye on my interests. The room is ready and available," he said and held out his hand.

Fiona scooted around on the bench and grasped his hand as she stood.

"You two have fun," Angie called, as Ransom guided Fiona away from the table. "We'll have dinner again soon!"

Once they stepped through the door that separated the playrooms from the lounge, Fiona expected to hear sounds coming from the closed doors. She heard nothing.

"Which room?" she asked.

"One, four, and seven are available. Which would you prefer?"

"Fa-fa-four," she stuttered.

He grinned. "Why four?"

She blushed.

"Come on Fi, it's me. Who can you tell anything to if not me?"

"The harness sounded intriguing," she said softly.

"Ah yes, I think we can have some fun with that," he said as they walked to the door for room four.

Ransom opened the door and Fiona stepped inside. It looked the same as it did the day they helped with the inventory. The room didn't show any signs of vandalism.

"How did you guys get it set to rights so fast?"

"The benefit of having this place staffed twenty-four-seven. The cleanup happened after RLS came in and photographed the scene and then fingerprinted should we decide to press charges if we ever learned who it was. The next day, we started on the repairs. The room was available again beginning yesterday."

"So, how does this work?"

"It's just like it always is between us, Fi. We go where the moment takes us," he quietly murmured before he kissed her.

One kiss led to another, which led to another. When they broke apart, both were gasping for air. Ransom's hands went to the hem of her shirt and tugged it over her head. Before she could reach for the buttons on his shirt, Ransom tugged her back into his arms and kissed her as he walked them to the bed.

Fiona broke the kiss when Ransom unhooked her bra.

"I need you," he whispered before he closed his mouth over one nipple.

He stripped her as he kissed and caressed her. Fiona unbuttoned his shirt and popped the snap and zipper on his jeans.

When he finally stepped back, she grabbed the waist of his jeans and shoved them, along with his underwear, down to his ankles.

"Get on the bed," he said as he finished removing his clothes.

Fiona didn't wait to see what he would do. She climbed up onto the bed.

Ransom crawled up the length of the bed to where she sat. He was everything she ever wanted.

"Lie back," he said, "and let me pleasure you."

When she rested back against the pillows, he spread her legs and, without preamble, licked where her legs joined. He continued the sweet torture until she was so close to exploding and then stopped. He kissed his way up her body and rolled them until she was on top.

As she rose above him, his erection slid inside her and she came just from the pressure of his entry. After she recovered, she started moving on him, determined to bring him as much pleasure as he had given her.

"I have fantasized about you on me like this since that time you blindfolded me. I love to see you move above me. Use my body to bring you to completion, baby. Then I'll use yours to bring on mine."

His words made her burst again. He grabbed her hips and continued to pump fast and hard up into her and bring on his own release as the waves of her orgasm faded.

She collapsed on top of him. He held her, gently rubbing her back.

"That didn't feel all that different from what we can do in your bed," she murmured.

"No, that wasn't. But just wait, the night is still young, and I have plans for you in that harness. Which I definitely don't have at home," he said in a deliciously dark tone as he grabbed her hips and pushed them down and ground her against him, reawakening her body in seconds.

27

———

"Just a minute!" Fiona yelled as she rose from the chair in the small room Ransom used as a home office. Someone was ringing the doorbell every two seconds. She'd been on the phone with the social worker at the home where her parents were while Ransom was in the pool swimming his daily laps. Shirley had found two facilities in Charleston that would meet the needs of her parents. One could take them both and was currently ensuring that they could keep them on separate floors, which had separate dining rooms and their own common areas, which would help avoid the fighting.

When the doorbell rang again, she swore. She had just stepped into the hall from the threshold. Another two seconds went by, and it rang again. "What in the hell?" she muttered. "Coming!" she yelled.

When it rang again, she sprinted to the door.

"What?" she demanded as she yanked the door open so hard the handle slipped from her hand and the door bounced off the doorstop and smacked her shoulder.

"Ow," she said, massaging her shoulder, looking at the person standing on the small porch.

Then Fiona recognized who she was looking at. It was the woman from the video. She had the hoodie on. She not only had hair almost the same as Fiona's, but she also looked enough like her that they could have been twins.

"Who are you?" Fiona asked.

"The one he is destined to be with," the woman said. "You need to leave. If you leave, everything will go back to the way it was. He was with me. He's supposed to be mine. We had a magical night together. I was everything he needed. Then you came along and ruined everything."

"Who are you?" Fiona repeated.

"It doesn't matter. You need to leave."

"And if I don't?"

"The boat explosion will look like child's play," the woman said.

"Fi!" Ransom called.

"No!" the woman shrieked as Ransom walked into the living room, still wet from the pool.

"What in the hell?" he asked. His gaze swinging from Fiona to the woman standing at the door.

"Ransom, tell her to go. She'll listen to you. You're mine. We have a connection. She messed it all up," the woman pleaded.

"Who are you?" Ransom demanded.

Fiona had a sudden hunch she knew where the woman had a magical night with Ransom.

"You're a member of Liaisons, aren't you?" Fiona asked.

"Yes."

"You were with Ransom there?" Fiona asked, venturing a quick glance at Ransom, who stood to her left.

"Yes. It was magical. I knew then we were meant to be together. He's mine. Not yours."

Fiona looked at Ransom then. She saw understanding in his eyes.

"Room four," he whispered.

"Yes. You took me in there."

"We were together twice, right?" Ransom asked.

"Yes. The first time you told me you didn't kiss on the lips. The second time you did. That was when I knew you felt what I did. If you broke your rule, it means we're meant to be."

"When did you get the tats?" Fiona asked and felt Ransom's surprised glance in her direction.

"How do you know they're recent?" the woman demanded, narrowing her eyes at Fiona.

"Because I know Ransom would have remembered them if you had them when you two had been intimate."

"I got them shortly after the last time we were together. Then Liaisons closed because of the fire, and I couldn't see him anymore."

"So, you learned where he lived?" Fiona asked.

"Yes," the woman said, gazing intently at Ransom. "I came by often but never could catch you at home. The first time I did, she was here too. I saw her grab you and kiss you. And then you pushed her away. I was so happy because I knew you did that because of how you felt about me. I hid when she stormed out of the house. I considered talking to you then, but decided it wasn't right. I came back the next day and the two of you were standing there," she paused and indicated the living room, "arguing and yelling. Then she grabbed you again and kissed you. Only this time, you didn't push her away. You pulled her closer. Then you made love to her," she said, anger filling her tone as her hateful gaze shifted back to Fiona, and her hands curled into tight balls at her sides. "You need to leave."

Still clutching her phone, Fiona tried to figure out a way to call the police.

"You blew up my boat?" Ransom asked, forcing the woman's attention back to him again.

"If I couldn't have you, she couldn't either," the woman said. "But that didn't work, which was just further proof that you and I are supposed to be together Ransom," she said. Then she looked at Fiona again. "You need to leave."

"No," Fiona said, determined she wouldn't take this anymore. Ransom belonged to her, not this woman. "You need to leave. Ransom has made his choice. He chose me."

"No," the woman said. Her rage transformed the word into a low, guttural noise. Then she pulled an object from her pocket and flicked it open. It was the knife, or at least it looked just like the knife, from the video of the person who destroyed room four.

Next thing Fiona knew, Ransom thrust her behind him and she tumbled to the floor. The jarring contact made her hit the button on her phone rapidly several times, which automatically called 911. It was a feature she never thought she would have to use. Now she was incredibly thankful for it.

"No!" Fiona screamed as the woman's arm continued in its downward motion. Horror shone on the woman's face. But she couldn't stop her momentum. The knife plunged into Ransom's left shoulder.

He roared in pain and shoved the woman away. Fiona suspected he was attempting to push her far enough beyond the door so they could close and lock it. It didn't work. The woman clutched the frame to stop her fall.

She could hear the firm voice of the 911 operator on the phone, wanting to know what the emergency was.

Fiona shouted, "Help! She has a knife!"

However, she never raised the phone to her ear. She didn't want the other woman to know the call had gone through and that maybe she would think someone was coming up behind her and turn around. Fiona hoped it would distract the woman. It failed. But the woman's sole focus was on Ransom.

"No! Ransom! No. I'm sorry. Why did you save her?" the woman asked, struggling to grab the knife.

Ransom was avoiding her hands. Fiona was unsure whether it was to hinder the woman from reclaiming the knife and going after Fiona, or if he feared that dislodging it would cause more damage to his shoulder.

"Stop moving. Let me remove the knife!" the woman shrieked.

"Who has a knife?" the 911 operator asked.

Fiona didn't respond. She knew they would dispatch a car to the location of her phone—in many ways it was great to live in such a technologically advanced era. She even thought she heard a distant siren.

"Stop. Let me help you, Ransom," the woman insisted again, moving further into the house now.

"No," he said, still dodging her hands.

When the woman's next step carried her within reach, Fiona extended her leg and tripped the woman. Fiona dropped her phone and, with a burst of strength unknown to her, she scrambled and laid on the woman and pinned her to the floor like she was a wrestler.

Yes, there definitely was a siren and it was getting louder.

"Ran!" Fiona exclaimed. "Grab my phone. It's connected to 911."

Fiona fixed all her attention on keeping the woman restrained. The woman's hands clawed back, attempting to reach Fiona. But thanks to Ransom's foot—which rested on one of the woman's wrists after he picked up the phone—there was only one hand now free. Fiona shifted her weight so less of it was on the side that Ransom controlled, and she pinned the remaining arm.

"Yes. I got stabbed. We have the person detained," Ransom said and then paused. "Yes, I need an ambulance."

Fiona tuned out the rest of his conversation and every other noise around her. She was resisting the urge to relax. Exhaustion was taking hold. The woman continued to fight against them and was shouting to be let up. Fiona concentrated solely on holding the woman down until the police arrived.

Hands brushed against her, and she flinched and then immediately pressed her weight down again.

"Fi, it's the cops. Let her go. They've got her," Ransom said against her ear.

Fiona registered hands holding the woman's shoulders now. She had been so preoccupied with guaranteeing that the woman couldn't get up, she'd failed to notice the officers' arrival. Boy, adrenaline did some strange things. How long had she kept the woman pinned?

She raised her gaze to Ransom, but before her eyes reached his face, she saw the knife lodged in his shoulder.

"It's okay," Ransom said. "Once you move, they'll control her. Then I'll go to the hospital and let them extract it."

"Why didn't you remove it?" Fiona said, getting to her feet with the help of one officer.

"I wasn't sure if it would do more damage."

Fiona missed everything else happening around them. All she could see was Ransom and there was a shadow encroaching on her peripheral vision. Then the trembling began.

"Sit down Fi," Ransom instructed. "I can't catch you."

Hands clasped onto her again—must have been one of the police officers because Ransom was still standing in front of her—and escorted her a few steps to the couch. She collapsed onto the cushions. The shaking eased a little. The darkness in her vision receded a fraction, but then the tears began.

Ransom sat beside her and wrapped his right arm around her. "It's okay, honey. Everything is alright."

"We need to take a report," an officer interrupted. "Do you feel well enough to do that now, or should we come to the hospital with you?"

"Yes," Ransom said, "come to the hospital."

Fiona heard silence as her world went black.

28

———

"She's fainted," Ransom told the officer.

"I've got her," one of the EMTs said. "Let's transfer her onto the gurney," he said to his partner.

"Can you take both of us at the same time?" Ransom asked as they loaded Fiona's limp body onto the waiting gurney. He was feeling a lot of pain now that the adrenaline was fading.

"Yes. We're in the multi casualty vehicle because all we knew was there was a stabbing. We were unsure how many people were involved."

"Good," Ransom said, following the EMT's to the vehicle.

They aided him onto the second gurney and then rolled him into the ambulance next to Fiona, who was still unconscious.

How had he forgotten about the woman from Liaisons? Easily, she didn't have tattoos when they had been intimate. He wondered what led her to get them after that. He remembered the second night they were together clearly now. He'd pretended she was Fiona. Sex with Fiona was always magical. He'd been so lost in the fantasy of being with Fiona that he unintentionally triggered something in the woman—and he still couldn't remember her damn name.

"Did you hear the name of the woman who did this?" he asked one of the EMTs.

"I only caught the first name. Kate," the EMT said as he assessed Fiona's vitals.

"Kate," Ransom reiterated and vividly recalled the initial time they had been together as well. What he hadn't realized was just how much she resembled Fiona until he had both in front of him at the same time. Their resemblance was so strong they could have been sisters.

He remained silent for the rest of the ride to the hospital. Damn, it was his second visit to a hospital within two weeks.

At least they had some answers. It didn't appear as though this was associated with Liaisons itself—just that was where he had met the woman. He had to inform Steven, Jon, and Mac. Damn! He'd forgotten his phone at home. That was okay. He had Fiona's in the pocket of his swim trunks. He knew at least Nicole and Jon's numbers were in her phone and likely Angie's. He could call Jon and let Jon tell the others.

At the hospital, they ran a few tests, did some scans, and concluded the knife had caused limited muscle and no tendon damage. It just hurt like hell, and they wanted to give him a strong antibiotic because there was no way of knowing what the knife had been in contact with before. During this time, Fiona awoke shortly after they had placed an IV in her hand.

"Shh," Ransom said when she called for him. "I'm right here. Look to your left, Fi."

When she did, he smiled.

"They still haven't removed it?" she asked, her eyes round and her face pale.

"They're about to. How are you doing?"

"A little energized," she said in a bewildered tone.

"Banana bag," he nodded at the IV. "Lots of good stuff in there to balance you and give you energy."

A nurse interrupted them, arriving to evaluate Fiona and a doctor to extract the knife from Ransom's shoulder. Just before they removed the knife, the nurse left the room to grab some extra dressing for the wound. The doctor quickly followed to consult on another case. Ransom took advantage of their absence to toss Fiona's phone to her.

"Text Jon and ask him to meet us at Liaisons tonight. We need to tell them what happened."

"Tonight? Really, you want to go to Liaisons tonight?"

"It's the easiest place to meet and fill them in on what we know."

"The police took the report?"

"Yes. They did while I was waiting for some scans and tests. They said they'll be in contact with you for your statement, but with what she did to me, they could press charges."

"Thank God!" Fiona said. "What time do you think I should tell him? I can text Nicole too."

Ransom roughly calculated the time it would take for them to finish up with him, discharge both of them, and get a ride home—likely with the help from one of the ride services. "Say eight just to be on the safe side," he suggested as he briefly glanced at the clock on the wall of their joint exam room that showed it was currently four o'clock.

The doctor and nurse returned, removed the knife, and stitched and bandaged his shoulder. It was on fire. During the process, Fiona kept quiet. When her phone made a noise, he watched her as she checked the message. She gave him a thumbs up. He understood her discreet sign meant that everything was ready for them to meet up and hopefully resolve the problems with Liaisons once and for all. Once they ended Kate's membership and implemented some added safety measures, Liaisons should operate as they envisioned, without all the tumultuous events of the preceding months. The only unresolved question was how Kate had known his door code, but if she had been following him for weeks, it was possible she had seen him enter it in on the keypad. He would have to be more cautious when he used the code box. And it was probably a good idea to change his code.

When the doctor discharged them, Ransom smiled at Fi. "Have I told you lately how much I love you?"

"I think so," she said, "but you could tell me again."

He paused and turned her to face him. "I love you. I'm sorry about what happened today. I understand if you want me to dissolve my partnership in Liaisons."

He didn't want to do that, but he knew it was something they had to address after today's events.

"No," she said, "but I'm going to follow Angie and Jon's relationship as an example. No playrooms for you without me."

He grinned. While the one time he took her, she had enjoyed the time they spent in the playroom delving into each other's fantasies, he expected her to ask him to leave after this.

"At least for now. We can revisit it when we become engaged," she said and turned away.

He smiled at her back. Well, that discussion would come sooner rather than later. He still had the ring he got for her all those years ago. He could never get rid of it. He would just have to find the right time to give it to her.

He jogged a few steps to join her and gently wrapped his right arm around her waist as they walked to the car they had called to whisk them home.

Epilogue

———

He took a spot across the room, concealed by the shadows on the far side of the bar. He liked the shadows; he lived in the shadows. It let him see and learn so much. He studied the three couples and one lone man sitting in one of the large, round booths. They laughed, talked, and sipped from various glasses. After a round of toasts, the four owners of Liaisons rose from the table and disappeared through the door that led to the playrooms. However, he was aware they weren't going into a playroom together. Most likely, their destination was the back office where they could discuss club business. He wondered what they needed to discuss now.

He observed the three women still sitting at the table. One blonde, one brunette, and one redhead. He knew them by name. Angela Bennett, Nicole St. James, and Fiona Campbell. He had fantasized about them since first catching sight of the three of them standing together all those weeks ago at Angie and Jon's engagement party.

As he watched, he concluded the three appeared to be very comfortable in each other's company. He hadn't expected that. Especially since Angie had intimate knowledge of the other two women's boyfriends. But then again, this was Liaisons. A lot of people practiced 'What happens here, stays here'. At least they were supposed to.

Of course, their easy conversation disappointed him. The flowers sent to Nicole, revealing the details about Steven and Angie, should have created some tension. From everything he saw right now, the two women appeared as if they were rapidly developing a friendship.

The four men returned. Mac, the only single one of the four, waved towards the ladies but went on to the bar. The other three men collected their women and escorted them back to the playroom area again.

He knew the three occupied three different rooms. He knew they weren't into anything remotely like his fantasy, where he had told all three women what to do to each other and him for hours on end. At the memory of the erotic fantasy, his cock jerked. He needed to find release. Glancing across the bar, he studied the occupants to see if anyone could live up to what he needed tonight.

His eyes settled on a woman alone at the bar. When he was about to stand and approach her, he saw Mac get to her first. She smiled at Mac. No woman had smiled at him like that since Mandy, damn it. She had been a good lay. Too bad she had run her mouth about them, he thought as he tossed back the contents of his glass and narrowly refrained from slamming the glass on the bar top. A second glass, filled, appeared in front of him. When he loosened his grip on the empty glass, the bartender whisked it away. Tim was good and could always gauge when he wanted a refill. Tim also knew he had never had over two drinks at the club.

He went back to studying the lounge, searching for someone that could hold his interest.

"Is this seat taken?"

Turning, he made eye contact with a blonde that was poured into a blood red dress. Lyra.

"No, it isn't," he said as he pulled out the stool so she could sit. "Could I order you something?"

"Whatever you're having will do," she said in her strangely accented voice.

He smiled. "Are you sure?"

"Why wouldn't I be?" she challenged with a raised, perfectly arched eyebrow.

"Tim, would you fix the lady an old-fashioned? Put it on my account."

"Sure. Ma'am, do you care which bourbon?"

"Whatever he has will do," she said, without looking at Tim.

Tim turned away to make the drink.

"Remind me," he purred, leaning close so only she could hear. "How long have you been a member here?"

"A few months," she said in a voice pitched just loud enough for him to hear and traced her fingertips along his thigh. "I joined right before the fire. You?"

"Oh, a little longer than that." He smiled. "Care to join me in the back where we can finish our drinks in private?"

"I was hoping for something a little less private," she pouted.

"We'll see," he said, standing. Lyra would do for now, and he would consider her request for something less private later. Maybe she'd go for the fantasy with two other women, he thought as he scanned the lounge area for any potential candidates.

The End

———

Keep reading for a sneak peek at Liaisons Book 4...

Sneak peek at Liaisons Book 4

At Liaisons the night Book 3 ends...

"What happened?" Mac asked.

"Hang on," Ransom said. "I'll explain when we're in the office."

Mac bit back the comment that there was no one around. Why did it have to wait? Mac had little patience, although it often looked like he had a lot. He was good at controlling his temper. At least he was now.

He followed Ransom, Jon, and Steven into the small room they used as an office. It held one conference table, multiple comfortable chairs encircling the table, and a large television on the wall for viewing security related things and presentations. It was all the room would hold after the renovations to the club. In truth, it was all they needed to conduct the club's business.

As they sat, Jon asked, "So things are going well with Fiona?"

Mac watched a smile slowly appear on Ransom's face.

"Yeah, things are going well," Steven chuckled softly.

Mac remained silent. There was no need to comment on it. He was only slightly jealous about the relationships the other three men had found. Oh, who was he kidding? He was very jealous. But now wasn't the time to dwell on that.

"They arrested Kate this evening," Ransom said.

"Who?" Mac asked. "And why?"

Ransom unbuttoned the first few buttons of his shirt and slid the left half away with his right hand, exposing a bandage stuck to the meaty part of his shoulder.

"She stabbed me," he said.

"Who is Kate?" Jon asked.

"Why did she stab you?" Steven inquired at the exact moment.

"A member here. I also have a feeling we uncovered who vandalized room four. I'd been with her there twice before the fire. I didn't recognize her because of the tattoos. She didn't have them the two times we were together."

"Her hair?" Jon asked.

"Damn close to Fiona's. I think it's her natural color, though. I don't think she was trying to make it look like Fi did it. She looks enough like her to be confused for Fi's sister if Fi had one. Kate's apparently been stalking me for a while. I'm pretty certain she saw me enter my code in the backdoor. That's how she got in that way. I figure she didn't want it documented that she came in the night she vandalized the room."

"What's her last name?" Mac asked.

"I don't know. I'll know once I get a copy of the police report. We can revoke her membership then," Ransom said.

"Was she trying to kill you?" Steven asked.

"She was trying to stab Fiona. I pushed Fi out of the way and Kate got me instead. The police have the knife. I think it was the same knife she used in the room, too."

"What about the fingerprints?"

Ransom shook his head. "I don't know. I'll follow up tomorrow. I imagine, though, it's because of a medical condition. I don't see her as the kind of person who would deliberately remove her fingerprints. I don't know what she does for a living, but her hands were smooth against my skin," Ransom said.

Mac asked, "What about your boat?"

"Kate too. Her reasoning was to take me out. She was willing to kill me because she didn't want anyone else to have me."

"I'll see if I can learn anything more tomorrow," Jon said.

"Do we want to press charges against her for room four?" Mac said. "Personally, I don't know if I want the cops involved in something here again."

"I agree with you there, Mac. They've been here too often over the past months. I'd like to get off their radar. But it might give her more jail time if we do. What did they charge her with?" Steven asked.

"I have absolutely no idea," Ransom admitted. "I hope they considered attempted murder after she confessed to us that she was the person behind the boat incident."

"More likely assault and battery with a deadly weapon," Mac said, "but I agree. Jon and I can follow up tomorrow. Until then, we can all contemplate filing charges for room four."

"Agreed," Jon said, rising. "For now, I have plans with Angie and a playroom."

"Same, only with Nicole," Steven said.

"I've already reserved room one," Ransom said. "It should be available now," he said, pushing back from the table.

"Looks like I need to find someone for the night," Mac said.

"I'm sure there are plenty of willing and able options out there," Ransom said.

Mac nodded as they filed out of the office and returned to the lounge. He casually made his way to the bar. He had all night and was debating on how he wanted to spend it.

After accepting a fresh drink from Tim, Mac caught sight of the woman sitting alone at the bar. When she made eye contact with him, he smiled. She smiled in return. Mac took that as the opportunity he desired and moved in her direction.

Liaisons Book 4–Coming 2025

Also by H. Elizabeth Austin

———

The Gibson Family Series

Falling for Ann

Temptation

Third Time's the Charm

Stay with Me

Until You

A Gibson Family Holiday

Because of You Series

Someone Like You

Led Me to You

In Your Arms (coming in 2025)

Liaison Series

Liaisons Book 1

Liaisons Book 2

Liaisons Book 3

Liaisons Book 4 (coming in 2025)

Milton Keynes UK
Ingram Content Group UK Ltd.
UKHW020823141124
451205UK00012B/695

9 798227 694508